"You Belong to Me."

His aqua eyes caressed her. "I'd meant to wait. But I think you need to be shown that you are very definitely mine."

"You don't own me. No one ever has or ever will." She backed away from him and came up short against the bed.

He shook his dark head. "It works both ways, sweetheart. Whether you want to admit it or not, we belong to each other. Come to me and make me live again," he whispered hoarsely as his lips came down on hers.

Retreat was impossible. Now she could no longer deny him anything. . . .

LAURIE PAIGE

would like to "go everywhere, try everything." With her family, she has camped at most of the national parks in the United States and she and her daughter have toured Europe on their own, staying at "bed and breakfast" inns and homes.

Dear Reader,

Thank you so much for all the letters I have received praising our SILHOUETTE DESIRE series. All your comments have proved invaluable to us, as we strive to publish the best in contemporary romance.

DESIREs feature all of the elements you like to see in a romance, plus a more sensual, provocative story. So if you want to experience all the excitement, passion and joy of falling in love, then SILHOUETTE DESIRE is for you.

I hope you enjoy this book and all the wonderful stories to come from SILHOUETTE DESIRE. If you have any thoughts you'd like to share with us on SILHOUETTE DESIRE, then please write to me at the address below:

> Jane Nicholls
> Silhouette Books
> PO Box 177
> Dunton Green
> Sevenoaks
> Kent
> TN13 2YE

LAURIE PAIGE
Gypsy Enchantment

Silhouette ❤ *Desire*

Published by Silhouette Books

Copyright © 1984 by Olivia M. Hall

First printing 1984

British Library C.I.P.

Paige, Laurie
  Gypsy enchantment.—(Silhouette desire)
  I. Title
  813'.54[F]   PS3566.A339/

  ISBN 0 340 35933 1

The characters and situations in this book are entirely imaginary and bear no relation to any real person or actual happening

This book is sold subject to the condition that it shall not, by way of trade or otherwise, be lent, re-sold, hired out or otherwise circulated without the publisher's prior consent in any form of binding or cover other than that in which this is published and without a similar condition including this condition being imposed on the subsequent purchaser.

Printed and bound in Great Britain for Hodder and Stoughton Paperbacks, a division of Hodder and Stoughton Ltd., Mill Road, Dunton Green, Sevenoaks, Kent (Editorial Office: 47 Bedford Square, London, WC1 3DP) by Richard Clay (The Chaucer Press) Ltd., Bungay, Suffolk

Gypsy Enchantment

1

The rain beat with relentless ferocity against the windshield as the Porsche pushed east on the interstate highway that would take Keri Thomas to New Orleans. The tropical storm, Zelda, had stalled in the Gulf south of the coast for three days, lashing the lowlands with gale-force winds and several inches of water.

Keri was making good time on the seven-hour trip from Houston, where she lived, to New Orleans, where she was considering opening another delicatessen and takeout gourmet shop. Glancing at the speedometer, she noticed that she was going seventy-five.

"Lead-foot," she said to herself accusingly as she let off the gas. Swinging south onto Interstate 10 at Baton Rouge, she realized that the storm was growing worse. Maybe it had finally decided to move inland.

She experienced a moment of fear as the car was buffeted from side to side. Gusts of wind constantly altered the course of the speeding auto, and she had to adjust the wheel accordingly.

At the next exit, she pulled onto the ramp, cruising the short distance to a truck stop tucked into the curve of a two-lane road. She parked, unsnapped the seat belt, and battling the weather, she threw open the door and raced inside the restaurant.

"Hi. Wet out there, isn't it?" the waitress said in friendly tones as Keri selected a booth and slid into the seat. The girl looked about ten years younger than her own twenty-eight years and was dressed in jeans and running shoes.

"Looks like it's getting worse," Keri commented with a smile as she accepted the menu. Her chic pantsuit was a designer model.

"Yeah, the twelve o'clock news said the storm was moving again. The eye will hit land late this evening." She left to get a glass of water and a set-up for the table.

Keri watched the lithe, swinging stride as the waitress moved across the tiled floor. Her eyes, as dark as flint and with a lucidity of expression that made them seem open to her innermost thoughts, filled with emotion that was so quickly gone that it might have been imagined. Her lips, medium full and stirringly sensuous, curled into a nostalgic smile.

When she had been eighteen, years and years ago, she, too, had worked in a restaurant, except that it had been an elegant place where casual clothes were unacceptable for workers or customers. That was where she had met Reid Beausan.

He had brought his dates in for elaborate meals complete with wine and the flaming desserts that were the dessert chef's specialty—until he had noticed her. Then he had come in alone several times, using the opportunity to talk to her and gain her trust before asking to drive her home. She should never have accepted, of course, but at eighteen, what does one know?

The waitress, who wore a plastic tag proclaiming her name as Debbie, approached and placed a paper placemat, a napkin and flatware on the table.

"It's a good thing this is November and the end of the rainy season." Debbie picked up the conversation where she had left off. "The weathermen have run through the whole alphabet of names for storms this season. I wonder if that's ever happened before."

Keri shook her head. "I don't know. I guess they'd have to start again with the A's if another one formed."

When she saw that the girl was ready with her pad and pencil, she ordered the plate lunch special and a cup of coffee. She was getting sleepy from the monotony of the drive. She checked her watch against the wall clock. It was just past two; plenty of time to reach New Orleans and get settled in for the night.

Thirty minutes later, she was on the road again. Worriedly, she surveyed the darkening sky and righted the drift of the car as the wind insistently pushed it off course.

As she neared the intersection of another major highway, her thoughts reverted to the past. After taking her home that first time, Reid had come to the restaurant almost every night, usually at quitting time. Waiting patiently with that smoldering, impatient look in his aquamarine eyes, he would watch while she finished setting up her tables for the next day's luncheon crowd. Then he would take her to his expensive car, but the time that she arrived at her apartment became later and later.

As she passed the turnoff, her eyes were drawn northward to the road that ran between Lake Pontchartrain and the smaller Lake Maurepas. There, past the canal that joined the lakes, was the small town named after Reid's family, Beausanville.

The Beausan mill was the main industry of the town, spinning thread from the cotton grown in the region. Cotton, rice, gas, oil and cattle all belonged to the Beausan empire. And the salt mines.

Don't forget the salt mines, she reminded herself, trying to hold on to the cynical thought, trying to ignore the small ache that throbbed suddenly in the old wounds of her heart.

Again her eyes were pulled from the highway to the winding road to the north that disappeared in the slashing rain. She didn't want to acknowledge that road or the past that it beckoned to life in her mind . . . old memories, old hurts. . . . Let them stay lost in the gray mists of yesterday, she told herself firmly. A veil of moisture formed over her eyes, and she blinked rapidly, angry at the display of useless emotion.

A question whose answer eluded her demanded again to know why she was going to Louisiana with the thought of opening another gourmet deli instead of searching out a place in Dallas, which would have been the most practical thing to do. Was she trying to go back to the summer she had been eighteen? No. There was nothing to go back to.

For a second, the mists of the past cleared, and she once again was facing Reid, a haggard, impatient-looking Reid, who said, "What are you doing here? I don't have time for you now." His frown had been preoccupied, hardly focused on her at all.

In the tragedy of his father's death, she had gone to him . . . to offer him the comfort of her presence, to share his grief, to simply be there for him . . . but he hadn't wanted her. He hadn't had *time* for her right then.

She had left his house, humiliated beyond anything she had thought possible, knowing without a doubt that she was merely a pastime for him, a plaything to be picked up when it was convenient . . . for him . . . and put down when it was not.

"I'll call you," he had said. They were the last words he had ever spoken to her, for she had gone to her bleak apartment, packed her clothes and headed west, not once stopping to look back. And she wouldn't start now, she vowed silently.

The wall of pain that rose in her was only an echo of the one she had felt ten years ago. Again she had to blink to clear her vision. The road in front of her was a gray ribbon on a backdrop of gray, making it difficult to concentrate on her driving.

Flexing her tired shoulders, she wondered how much of the success she had achieved stemmed from the stabbing mortification of that day. It seemed impossible that she had been so foolish—so in love, so starry-eyed, dreaming her Cinderella dreams.

Oh, well, life was like that. "Chicken one day and feathers the next" was what old Spencer, the Cajun who delivered fresh seafood to the restaurant, had commented once when she had helped him with his unloading. He had been her friend.

The wheel was nearly wrenched from her hands, bringing her attention back to the slippery road. There was very little traffic—which was understandable. Nobody but an idiot would be out in this. Ruefully, she admitted that she should have waited until next week to travel. She could have changed the Friday appointment with the real estate agent to Monday or Tuesday easily.

GYPSY ENCHANTMENT

But she was always compelled to get things done. Hence, this drive on a wet and windy Thursday. Crazy, really crazy.

The Porsche veered sharply toward the side of the road. As she swung the wheel to correct the motion, a movement at the corner of her eye brought her attention to the median. A large dog came running across the grass and up on her side of the road.

Reacting instinctively, Keri jerked the car hard toward the right. She felt the tires on that side drop off the edge of the pavement, then the whole situation was somehow out of her hands. The vehicle careened, lurching wildly, down the grassy bank and across a shallow drainage ditch. Then there was a rush of fence that immediately disappeared and then a forest of trees coming at her.

Keri covered her face with her arms as the Porsche snapped the tall, thin pines with a crackling sound like a forest fire, an inferno of noise. She felt the pain in her head first; it moved to her shoulder and then her chest. A burning, tearing pain that made it impossible to breathe for long minutes.

When she came to, several dimly perceived bodies moved across her vision. The rain that had been falling on the windshield now struck her face. She raised a hand to hold it off. A groan was torn from her lips.

"Reid," she whimpered. "Reid."

"We'll get you out soon," a masculine voice assured her.

There was a consultation on the best way to remove her from the tangled sheets of crumpled metal. Someone worked on the door with a crowbar, then hands reached in for her. She passed out as they carefully extracted her from the wreckage.

Later, she heard a siren, a light was flashed into her

eyes, first one, then the other, and sometime after that, she was aware of white and green figures floating around. A hospital, she realized.

"Was she wearing a seat belt?"

A policeman writing his report, she thought as she became conscious yet again.

"I don't know," someone answered.

Oh, God! she cried silently. That voice! She opened her eyes, saw the hazy glow of a streetlight against the black night. She turned her head and looked into aquamarine eyes.

"Hello, gypsy," Reid said.

"Go away, Reid," she warned in what she thought was a firm, authoritative voice. "You're not my lover anymore."

Chuckles followed that statement, and the doctor remarked, "Plenty of fight left in this one." He efficiently looked her over.

She closed her eyes tightly as the relentless pain claimed her, making her weak, calling her into that netherworld.

For the next three days, the image stayed with her: aquamarine eyes, dark, straight hair—not as dark as the black cloud of long, curling hair that she had—thick eyebrows that were almost straight across and long, curving lashes that framed the coolly distant gaze of those unusual eyes.

Reid still wore his hair without a part. Cut rather short, it grew naturally from the crown of his head toward his face, like a well-fitted helmet of some new-technology material that was incredibly soft but strong.

His six feet, two inches tapered from football shoulders to slim hips and long, masculine legs of great strength. She knew his form so perfectly. On his right buttock was a scar where, as a child, he had swiped his fishing knife on his pants to clean the blade. In the small of his back grew a scanty line of short, dark hairs along his spine. His legs and chest were thickly covered by a glossy mat of dark hair that she had loved to stroke.

She lifted a hand and it was taken into a warm clasp.

"What day is this?" she asked the large figure that bent over her bed.

"Sunday," he answered.

She had loved Reid's voice from the first moment she had heard it. It was deep, a bass voice, and it held all the serenity in the world in its smooth tones. It said there was no situation he couldn't handle; he was always in control.

"Turn on the light," she requested.

His strong features leaped out of the shadows when he complied. Her dark eyes explored his face, comparing her vivid memory of him with what she saw now.

His jawline was strong, almost cruel in repose. She once told him he could play the role of a heavy on TV if he ever needed a job. He had punished her laughter by rubbing the rasp of beard that he always had against the tender skin of her abdomen. Then they had made love.

A sharp contraction twisted her insides into a knot as memory became reality for an instant—his lips on hers, on her throat, coaxingly gentle on her breasts, her innocent breasts that had known no man's touch before his.

"What is it?" Reid asked, sensing her unrest.

"I hurt." Her hand went to her pounding head where a hammer beat with continuous, steady strokes.

"You have a concussion. Rest. Things will be better soon."

She pushed the weakness of pain from her, and her flint-dark eyes became caverns that let no light of emotion out. "Life doesn't get better; it just goes on and on."

His lips, so firm but so sweetly enticing, touched the corner of her mouth. "It will be better from now on. My word of honor." And he smiled at her as if he knew a wonderful secret.

Closing her eyes, she shut him out, but she couldn't shut off the sensation in the spot where he had kissed her. Reid was different, she thought, from the twenty-four-year-old she had known ten years ago. His self-confidence had deepened into a masculine assurance with no overt assertiveness; he was a man who knew his own strengths, who had been tested by time and experience and had come out on top.

And so had she. She, too, had survived all that life had thrown at her. Now she was strong and self-contained. Careful of the tube that dripped some colorless liquid into her arm, she laid her left hand on her stomach and placed her right hand over it. Wincing a little as she yawned, she drifted into sleep.

To the man standing beside her, she looked fragile, close to death with her pale face and lips that had worn a blush of roses when he had last kissed them. Her wild gypsy hair was in a tumble on the pillow, one swatch cut away in order to sew up the wound in her scalp.

Her lung had been punctured and she had nearly died.

On his way home from a business trip in New Orleans, he had heard her name on the radio as the accident report was given along with the warning to motorists of deteriorating road conditions. Unable to believe that it was she, he had, nevertheless, made a U-turn at the next crossroad and headed back to town, keeping his speed at a sedate fifty-five. She had apparently been going seventy or eighty when she went off the road, and he wondered where she was going and why it was so important for her to get there so fast. What had her life been like during the past ten years? Who had lived it with her? She wore no wedding ring. For a second, his strong jaw tensed and his eyes glittered dangerously. Then he turned and quietly left the room.

On Tuesday, Keri was moved from the intensive care unit to a private room. She assumed that this meant she was going to live. Her smile was sardonic as she watched the nurse bustling around, getting her settled.

Reading the name tag, she discovered her nurse was Mrs. Baker, an LPN. Maybe everyone should wear a name tag, she mused. What would hers say? Keri Thomas, orphan? Keri Thomas, entrepreneur? She grinned at the thought, and Mrs. Baker, folding the sheet neatly at the foot of the bed, smiled back. The woman had the most beatific smile; her whole face joined in.

A knock on the door heralded the delivery of a basket of flowers. "Oh, my, now isn't that pretty!" Mrs. Baker stopped her tasks to admire the gift. She cleared a space on the night table and placed the bouquet there, handing the card to Keri.

"I'll bet it's from the young man who's been hanging around, getting in everybody's way and asking a hundred questions about your health since you were brought in," she said, beaming as she waited for Keri to confirm her guess.

Inside the card was only an initial, R.

"Yes, it's from Reid," Keri murmured for the nurse's benefit. Arrogant lout, was her personal reaction. An R. Like he was some kind of king. She waited until Mrs. Baker left before looking at the flowers closely.

Their beauty took her breath away. Gazing at them,

she was wafted backward in time to summery days of golden hues. White spider mums, big yellow mums and glorious bronze mums made up the arrangement along with the usual ferns and greenery. She plucked one bronze mum from its bed. Cupping it in both hands, she stared at its petals intently. It was like holding a fluffy ball of burnished sunshine.

Did he remember, after all these years, that these were her favorite?

Feeling eyes on her, she glanced toward the door. Reid stood there with a suitcase—she recognized it as one she had taken on her trip—in one hand and a basket of fruit and small cans of fruit juice in the other. A box of candy was tucked under his arm.

"Did you buy out the store?" she asked, managing to keep her voice light and teasing. A fine greeting after all these years, but then, she hadn't had much experience in renewing acquaintances with old lovers. She replaced the elegant flower.

"Only the fruit section," he responded easily, his eyes rapidly skimming her slight figure in the coarse hospital gown. "There wasn't that much of a selection. Mostly apples and bananas, a few pears, some seedless grapes. I brought juice instead of oranges. Less messy, I thought."

"You think of everything," she complimented, her tone wry, her smile nicking only the corners of her lips.

He checked the room and then came around the bed to place the fruit and candy on the rolling table which was supposed to hold her meal trays conveniently over her lap. He placed the case in the small closet.

"Do you like your room?" he asked in his serene tones.

Like a calm tide rolling in from the depths of the sea, she thought. "If I didn't, would you have it changed?"

GYPSY ENCHANTMENT

She glanced at the pale beige wall and the complementary floral wallpaper in soft shades of orange and gold and beige.

"Naturally." He focused on her attire. "You have a very pretty nightgown in your case. Would you like to put it on?" His grin was seductive, softening the line of his jaw and adding crinkles at the corners of his eyes. "I'll be glad to help." The lines were deeper in his face than they'd been the last time she'd seen him but his added maturity only made him that much more attractive.

She tried to decide quickly on her position. Should she assume an air of modesty and decline his half-mocking offer? He expected her to say no.

Modesty seemed somewhat ridiculous in the light of their past association. Perhaps she should be the experienced woman of the world, permitting him to help, letting him see that his presence had no effect whatsoever on her.

A slight tremor invaded her tummy. Could she carry that off? Already she was reacting to his powerful influence. Startled, she realized that she wanted him to kiss her, to hold her and make the hurt go away.

With a low laugh, he retrieved the bag and rummaged through it, coming up with the gold satin gown trimmed in bronze lace and the matching peignoir.

At her slight frown, he said, "Don't be shy, gypsy. I've had enough of looking at you in that rag you're wearing." He wrinkled his nose at her, the expression teasing but engaging at the same time.

He handed her the gown and considerately turned his back while she stripped out of the hospital sack and carefully slipped into her own outfit. At her murmur, Reid turned and held the thin robe for her, then tied it at her bosom and waist, making attractive bows from the long, thin ribbons.

"You would make a good lady's maid," she said, hiding her reaction to the feel of his hands on her. Mostly they stirred up old feelings and sensations that she didn't want to remember, she confessed to herself. "Did you bring my brush and comb, by any chance? My hair is a mess."

"Um-hmm," he replied. "Better let me do it. You have several stitches on one side. They had to cut the hair away, but I think we can hide the bare spot with a middle part."

"That must be why they didn't give me a mirror. The shock would probably be too great," she quipped.

Reid's hands went to her hair, starting from the tangled ends and working toward her scalp with the large-toothed comb until the locks were free of snarls once more.

"Here," he said, holding up a mirror from her suitcase and tilting her head so she could see her injury.

"Yuk," she said, eyeing the jagged line and red scalp.

Reid flicked her short, slightly upturned nose before tossing the comb back in the case. He removed her lipstick from the zippered makeup bag. "Pucker up," he advised. Rolling the lipstick up, he patted it on her waiting lips, nodded at his handiwork and put it away. Then he removed the luggage from the bed.

"How do you feel?" he asked. His eyes raked her from head to foot and back as they had done when he first came in. It was as if they could penetrate her calm facade with their glacier beam.

Her smile brought a dimple into play in each cheek. Lifting her small chin with its suggestion of a cleft, she returned his gaze with a lucid-but-opaque stare from eyes that were shiny and dark, like material forged deep in the heart of a volcano. Touching the bandage beneath her gown, she told him she was fine. "Except it hurts when I breathe deeply."

He hooked an expensive shoe on the crossbar of a straight chair and pulled it close to the bed and sat down. "Your lung was punctured. Just missed your heart."

"I'll have a scar?" she asked, fingering the spot above her left breast.

"It won't bother me," he assured her with male logic. "Don't talk. You're supposed to rest a lot."

Settling back against the pillows, she let herself enjoy the sight of his maleness without dwelling on what it did to her to have him close like this . . . and her in bed!

"I had an appointment—"

"I saw it in your purse, which I have, by the way. I called the guy in New Orleans and explained what happened. I'm afraid the property has already been leased by someone else."

"Oh, well," she said, shrugging off his implied concern philosophically. "Something else will turn up."

"I did some prying into your affairs." He quirked one brow.

"What did you find out?" She was amused at his apologetic attitude. It was certainly unusual for him.

A grin quickened across his face. "You're quite an entrepreneur these days. You've been busy the past ten years."

It was his first reference to the time that had elapsed since they had last met. Only the use of his pet name for her, "gypsy," and the command for her not to be shy had indicated their past association.

She nodded without answering. She was beginning

to feel the effects of the change in rooms and of his visit as a weariness seeping into her bones.

Reid stood, his height dominating her prone position. "I've contacted your insurance company about your car. The Porsche was totaled. I also talked to your office in Houston a couple of times. Your attorney is readying a report for you. Seems to be some trouble brewing. He wouldn't explain it to me, violation of confidence, I think." He waved a hand to show that he understood her lawyer's position about disclosing her business.

"Yes, thank you. For everything." She dredged up a smile. "You don't have to come anymore, Reid. I can take care of things now. You probably have a jealous wife at home," she joked.

He shook his head, and she experienced the power of his brilliant gaze directly on her. "No wife, past or present." His eyes narrowed to glittering slits. "I once let a good thing get away from me by my own carelessness. I won't let that happen again."

He pushed the chair over to the wall, then returned to the bed and bent to her. His lips, wonderfully sensual against her own, roamed with familiarity over her mouth.

It was a brief kiss, strangely incomplete but filled with promise. She squeezed her eyes shut, feeling weak and helpless.

"I'll see you later," he said and was gone, leaving the full force of his male potency behind him to haunt her even after she fell asleep.

Reid kept his word, coming to see her every day, bringing her a gift each time in spite of her protests. She improved rapidly, lengthening the time she sat up or went for walks down the long corridors by several minutes each day.

Before the accident, she'd been in good shape because she belonged to a gym in Houston and exercised there four or five times a week when she was home. Soon the pain in her head went away entirely, and her lung was mending without complications. She began to question the doctor about going home. She had been in the hospital for over two weeks, and her business affairs needed attention. She had called her attorney to discuss buying out her partner's share in the deli business. Mack, her partner, was quite agreeable. It was his wife who was causing the difficulty. Keri was anxious to get home and iron out the situation.

Finally, the doctor agreed to let her go on Wednesday, the day before Thanksgiving. That was only two days away, she realized with relief. Then she could go home and put all this behind her.

Her plans didn't get off the ground. Reid, with the surgeon's support, insisted that she couldn't go back to Houston yet. She was still weak, they argued; she could easily get pneumonia if she became fatigued.

"I'm not letting you go," Reid said in private after her stormy battle with him and Dr. Denney.

"What do you mean?" Her mouth tucked in angrily at the corners. She wasn't used to being contradicted or following orders.

His hands, long-fingered and artistic, spanned her shoulders, curving over the bones and muscle in graceful arches. "I'm going to take you home with me. You need looking after until you're completely well." He was quietly adamant.

Keri found herself wanting to yield to the gentleness of his touch; she wanted to have someone who really cared, she thought, then rebuked the foolish notion. "I can look after myself. I have for years. . . ."

"Not this time," he said, coolly insouciant as he took over. "You need to be near the hospital, just in case. And"—he leaned over her to gaze solemnly into her eyes—"I need to know you're all right. I'd go out of my mind with worry if you went back to Texas."

Troubled, she bit on her inner lip as the familiar weakness washed over her. She had to admit that she was far from healthy yet. "Perhaps I should stay close," she began. "An apartment..."

"No," he said. "You can't stay alone. At my house there'll be people to watch after you while I'm at work."

"I don't need watching after," she told him angrily.

"Yes, you do," he contradicted her.

The top half of her bed was raised in order to let her sit upright, and she pressed backward into the pillows, trying to evade his grip. He let her go and sat on the side of the bed, his thigh resting against the curve of her hip, bringing warmth and a strange, glowing comfort by its hard, male presence.

Another wave of fatigue caught her in its clutch, and she brought trembling hands to her tummy as if to hold the illness at bay. Her head was starting to hurt, and the area around her left lung ached.

"I intend to have my way in this," he added after watching the expression of pain cross her face.

"And what Reid wants, Reid gets, right?"

"Right." His voice was quiet in contrast to her mutinous tones.

She saw that he wouldn't be put off. Sighing, she accepted the inevitable. As he said, there would be people at his house—it wasn't as if they would be alone. And what difference did it make where she stayed to convalesce?

Hardening herself to absolute frigidity and ignoring the heat that seeped from his leg to hers, she finally nodded. "All right, I'll stay with you. . . ."

Her words were taken from her mouth by his kiss, his hands sliding around her back in the first overt action he had taken with her. Her thoughts were frantic before she decided to coldly wait him out, to let him see that she was unaffected by his tactics. He would see that she was no longer that naive eighteen-year-old who had trusted him, who had given all of herself without reservation.

His fingers moved along her spine as if he were playing a melody on an exotic instrument. A small shiver passed through her. He lifted her in his arms and sat in the one large, comfortable chair in the room and cuddled her close. His hand stroked her hips through the satin fabric of her gown and robe. The bony ridge of his nose frankly nuzzled along her neck as he strung kisses on her throat like invisible jewels that created a glow in her skin. He inhaled deeply.

"You smell so good," he groaned. "I've wanted to taste and smell and touch you ever since I walked into this hospital and saw that it was really you and not some stranger."

Lifting his dark head, he pierced her with his gaze and she felt her coldness dissolving a little bit more. "Do you have any idea of the agony I went through following that announcement on the radio?" he demanded, almost accusing her of having the accident just for the pleasure of tormenting him.

"Reid," she began on a reasonable note, alarmed by the fierce emotion in his aquamarine eyes. "Reid, why are you doing this? There's nothing deader than an old love affair. Let it go," she ordered sharply.

He placed hot kisses along her cheek, her temple, on

her eyelids and down her nose, searching for her mouth. "No, gypsy, it's not dead. We weren't through with each other before . . ."

She strained from his seeking lips, her resistance slipping with each breath she drew. "Yes, we were through," she insisted.

His long, tapering fingers massaged along her waist, closing over her hip bone with remembered intimacy. His warm breath brought answering sensations to the skin of her face, which grew heated from his touch.

"Why did you leave?" he whispered hoarsely.

"There was nothing to stay for."

"For this," he said. "And this." His hand moved over her, closing carefully on her breast while his mouth closed over her lips, seeking entry there with his forceful tongue until she opened her mouth to the invasion of his.

His palm made tiny circles that brought the hard pebble of her nipple into sharp, thrusting display through the gold material. His tongue stroked and explored in all the old remembered ways until hers joined in the erotic foray.

The coldness was gone and a warmth spread throughout her small-boned, slender form as she responded as she always had to Reid's touch and his kisses.

He stroked the dark, curling mass of hair from her face, pausing to look into her flint-dark eyes, which showered sparks over him as she became aroused under his caresses. He smiled slightly before ducking his head to return to the exploration of her yielding mouth.

As always, the female in her reacted to the male in him. Two parts that made a whole. It had been this way from the first kiss between them. She had thought it was love. But it wasn't.

And remembering that fact, she twisted her head from his pervasive influence. "Stop it," she ordered. "I'll only go home with you . . . if . . ."—she steadied her shaky voice—"if you promise to leave me alone."

His smile wasn't triumphant as she had expected, but it was tender, gentle and somehow understanding. She had the impression that if she stayed in his arms, then everything would forever be right in her world.

Such fantasies! she scoffed to herself.

He carried her to the hospital bed and placed her on it. "I'll be careful with you," he said with a definite commitment in the words.

After he left, she considered her capitulation. So okay, she would spend Thanksgiving at his house—there would probably be lots of relatives around. Then she would go home.

How many relatives did he have? She tried to remember the newspaper write-ups when his father had died. There were no other children, but Reid had a couple of aunts from his father's side, some uncles in Texas from his mother's family. She knew that his mother had died three years ago. Not very many relatives for so powerful a family, but still, a few. Which was more than she had.

On Wednesday, promptly at ten o'clock, Reid came for her, tossing a package from Neiman-Marcus, Texas's most elegant department store, in her lap when he came into the room. Inside was a pantsuit identical to the one she had been wearing when she had the wreck.

She held up the heathery green, lightweight wool material and the teal blouse of pure silk, staring at it in surprise. It was exactly her size. "How . . . how did you . . ."

"I called, described what I wanted and told them the

size from the old one and they sent it out to me," he explained, pleased with his gift.

He was like a small boy with a present for his mother, she thought, resenting his intrusion into her life. He took it for granted that she would accept his present.

"Please," he said, reading her thoughts.

"Thank you," she returned not very graciously.

Mrs. Baker bustled in, looking like a miniature football player until she smiled her angelic smile. "Need some help? My, isn't that pretty." She spotted the clothes spilling over Keri's lap. Holding the door, she cast an inquiring eye on Reid, who retreated to the hall at the unspoken command.

Keri suppressed a laugh as he hurried out. Mrs. Baker closed the door and came over to the amused young woman. With quick, sure movements, she helped Keri out of her gown and into underclothes and then the attractive, expensive outfit.

Her suede shoes of forest green were wearable, having only gotten damp in the accident, not damaged. She slung the matching shoulder-strap purse over her arm and was ready to go. Mrs. Baker opened the door, and Reid followed her across the room to grab her suitcase.

The nurse looked over the papers to see that they were in order before she brought a cart in to load Keri's flowers and gifts for the trip downstairs.

"Keri," the woman read the name aloud. "That's so pretty. Do you know what it means?"

Keri shook her head, sure that Mrs. Baker was going to tell her. She didn't think it meant anything. Somebody from the state social service had picked it out.

"I just finished a tour in the pediatric wing. Never had any children of my own, but I've helped name hundreds." She smiled broadly at them. "Keri means 'homeward bound.' It's a gypsy word. 'Ker' is gypsy for 'home,' you know." She beamed at the young couple.

"No, I didn't know," Keri said slowly, a tightening in her chest spreading upward to her throat with a strange ache.

"That's apropos," Reid interrupted, his sea-colored eyes sparkling. "For that's where we're going. Home."

In a few minutes, he and Keri were driving off in his car while Mrs. Baker waved an energetic goodbye from the steps of the hospital.

2

The temperature was in the low seventies, and the sky was crystal bright, a far cry from that stormy Thursday. She grimaced as she thought of the accident.

"What's the face for?" Reid asked sociably.

"I was just thinking—here I was in New Orleans for three weeks and all I saw was the inside of a hospital."

He laughed, the rich sound blending with the sunshine and smell of flowers piled in the back seat of his expensive sedan. "I'll take you back and give you a tour of the town after Christmas," he promised.

Chills chased themselves along her spine. "What makes you think I'll be around that long?"

His fascinating eyes cut sharply toward her, then back to the highway. "I'll guarantee it, gypsy. Your roaming days are over." He was suavely confident, which irritated her.

"You can't go back to what used to be, Reid." Her softly spoken words carried an unmistakable warning.

"No," he sighed heavily, "but you can go forward from this moment. And that's what we're going to do."

His hand reached across the space between them to clasp hers in a light embrace. "Sit close to me," he invited.

"No, thanks. I've already been in one accident recently," she replied dryly.

"Umm, you're right. We'll wait."

A few miles along the road, past the flood control spillway between the lake and the Mississippi River, Reid turned right, going north to the land between the lakes. Instead of driving straight to his house, however, he turned again, arriving at a small promontory of land next to Lake Pontchartrain. He switched off the engine.

"What are we stopping for?" she demanded. She didn't want to be alone with him; she was safer among people.

"A picnic," he explained.

Lithely he swung his tall frame out of the vehicle, opened the trunk and brought out a large paper sack. Then he came around to her side, opened her door and, giving her his hand, helped her alight. At a picnic table next to the leveed edge of the water, he seated her and then began spreading the contents of his parcel on the concrete surface.

Keri gasped as he placed a distinctive black rectangular cardboard box with silver embossing on it in front of her. With arrogant assurance that the silver outline of a spoon was enough to identify the shop, she had had the box designed without lettering.

"Where did you get this?" she asked.

"From your shop in Houston, of course. The Silver Spoon Gourmet Shop." He supplied the full name of her takeout speciality store. "I had the lunches flown in yesterday. I took the liberty of supplying my own wine." He placed glasses on the table, opened a carafe of rosé and poured them each a generous amount.

"Am I allowed to drink wine?" She arched a fine, dark brow at him.

"I checked with the doctor. He said a glass with your meal would be okay." His thick, straight brows lifted slightly as he held a glass toward her for a toast.

She accepted the fragile glass and sipped the wine, her eyes roaming the lake, picking out familiar landmarks from her past. In the distance, the causeway neatly split the lake into halves. Twenty-six miles long, it conveniently connected the north shore with New Orleans on the south shore.

Unexpected emotion surged through her, leaving a sense of disquiet in its place. A restlessness pervaded her spirit. She realized that she had missed this swampy bayou country during her years in the flat plains of Texas. She hadn't known that . . . or she had refused to recognize it.

She opened her box lunch when Reid sat down opposite her and opened his. Inside were slices of meat pâté served on thin slices of French bread, a vegetable pâté, a salad and a fruit tart, all kept cool inside the padded, insulated cardboard. This was the most costly of the gourmet lunches served in her shop.

Later, after they finished and Reid had cleared the table, tossing the elegant debris in a nearby trash barrel, he sat next to her, a businesslike firmness in his countenance.

"Now," he informed her, "we are going to talk."

"Haven't we been doing that?" she hedged.

"No, we've been chattering. For three weeks, you've evaded my attempts to delve into your life, but now I want some answers."

Ignoring the warmth of his nearness, the pressure of

his shoulder and thigh against hers, Keri folded her hands together on the hard tabletop and waited. Each time Reid had tried to question her, she had turned his inquiry aside with light quips and evasive answers. He was having no more of that. She scrambled through her mind for answers that would satisfy him and yet disclose nothing too personal. Her life was her own; she wasn't going to share it with anyone.

"Why did you leave?" he asked, spearing her with his bright gaze that would drive the truth from one more susceptible than she to its piercing charm.

"Are we back to that? I think we've been through this." Her soft laughter was mocking.

"You packed up and left without a word," he accused.

"And you have a convenient memory, recalling only the facts as you see them. You told me to get out, remember? You said you didn't have time for me." Her voice was calm, containing no trace of self-pity. She was as in control of her emotions and mental processes as he was.

"I came looking for you. . . ."

"When?"

"A month or so later. When I couldn't find you, I hired a detective agency. You disappeared without a trace. Where did you go?"

She grinned at him. "To Corpus Christi." There, let him figure that one out.

"I suppose you had a reason?" He paused, but she only cast one cool glance at him and returned to her study of the waterfront. "Do you realize how hard it is to trace someone who has no ties, no connections with anyone or anything that you can discover?"

"Umm," she murmured noncommittally.

His hand settled on the back of her neck, the tapering

fingers caressing her skin with sensuous strokes under the flowing mass of her hair.

"When the detective started questioning me on your life, I found out I knew nothing about you . . . and I would have sworn I knew everything." He laid his right hand on the table and stuck out his forefinger. "One, I knew you had been born in Baton Rouge. Two," he counted, "you were an orphan. Three, you worked as a waitress. Three hard facts, the sum total of all I knew of you."

"You knew my age," she reminded him.

"Not until I talked with the restaurant owner. I thought you were about twenty-one. I found out you were eighteen and your birthday was in May. That's not much to go on."

A thread of anger wound its way through his words, and Keri was pleased that he had been frustrated. It wasn't often that a Beausan was thwarted, she surmised. The experience had probably been good for his character.

"Why Corpus Christi?" he suddenly demanded.

She swallowed the last sip of wine. "My people were from there." She twirled the long stem between her fingers, a sign of nervousness. His questions were getting too personal.

"Tell me about it. Please," he added, his voice matching the serene lap of the lake water against the steep shore.

Her eyes stayed on some point in the far distance as she explained. "I knew my mother's maiden name, and even though the police hadn't been able to trace any relatives for either of my parents, I guess I still hoped to find some. Anyway, I went to Corpus Christi and asked around until I found some people who remembered them from high school."

"And?" His fingers tightened on her neck.

Pulling from his grasp, she shook her head. "And that's all. I went to the school and saw their pictures in the high school annuals. They looked nice. My mother was pretty. They came from poor families—farmers and factory workers. And it seemed to be true—there were no living relatives."

Her parents had left Texas and come to Louisiana so that her father could work on an offshore oil rig. Apparently, they had been here a little over a year when the auto accident occurred. He had died instantly and Keri's mother had lived long enough to give birth to the premature infant.

Keri's expression became closed, guarded, as if she were determined not to betray any emotion. She would give Reid the bare facts, that was all.

"How long did you stay there?"

"About three months."

"Where did you go after that?"

Sighing with exasperation at his persistence, she continued her recital. "I headed up the coast and drifted around for a while." She shrugged to show it hadn't been important. "Then I went to Houston. I figured I'd have more opportunity to get rich in a large, bustling city."

Both his arms closed around her. "We searched for over a year," he murmured, his bass voice going husky and very soft. "All we could find were tiny pieces of your past, nothing of your future."

She grinned saucily at him. "Most people have an inherited future. Like you and your salt mines. Being an orphan has its advantages; you're free to make your own future. You can even make up a past to go with it."

She placed a hand over his fingers that were spread

out over her abdomen, kneading gently into the flat wall of muscle where a fire was beginning to burn.

"I missed you, Keri," he said, using her name for the first time. The seriousness of his tone brought goose bumps to her scalp.

"I was a recreation for you, nothing more." She shook her head, the curls bouncing wildly at the action. "You can't treat a person like that, Reid As if I were a bag of golf clubs to be stored in a closet until you had the time or desire to play again. I won't take that from anyone." She maintained the careful balance of her voice so that no remembered anguish bled through.

His hand tightened for a second. Then he released her and swung one long leg over the stone bench, straddling it. He pulled her into the warm shelter of his body as if to protect her from past hurts, his arms firmly holding her in close contact but careful of her still-tender wounds.

"I never thought of you as recreation. You were . . . a friend." The strange, husky sadness of his voice tugged at her compassionate nature. His smile was fleeting. "A warm, laughing companion. I found it relaxing to be with you . . . more so after we started making love."

A blush flowed up her neck and into her face in spite of her trying to will it into oblivion.

"May I tell you about that day, Keri? Will you listen?"

He waited for her hesitant nod before resuming. His nearness was eroding the aloof distance she had placed between them in the hospital. It had been a mistake to let him talk her into coming home with him.

"My father wasn't cold in his grave, hell, he wasn't even in his grave, when my uncles started pouring in like a pack of wolves hoping to get in on the kill. They wanted to talk my mother into letting them control her money. But my father had left me in charge. That was a lot of responsibility for a twenty-four-year-old; to take the reins of a far-reaching business empire and to console my mother and two aunts, to arrange for the funeral and hold off the wolves at the same time."

Keri remembered how tired and pale he had looked when he came into the study at his home where she waited for him.

With one finger, he turned her chin so that she faced him now. "When you appeared, it seemed you were one more of the pack, out for what you could get, catching me at a weak moment."

She wrenched her head from his touch. "How could you think that?" Her voice was almost inaudible, trembling with anger.

"I know," he said sadly. "It wasn't until later that I realized that you had never asked anything of me that entire summer. You never hinted for gifts or asked to be taken to expensive places. You came to comfort me, didn't you?"

She shrugged. "I don't know. It doesn't matter."

Reid hadn't come to her or called. She had read of his father's death in the paper, and her heart had been stricken. How much worse to know and love a father and then lose him, she had thought, than to have never known one at all. You don't miss what you have never had, or so the theory went.

A gripping weariness washed over her, leaving her with a sick weakness. "Reid, I'm tired . . ."

He stood up. "We'll go home now. I just wanted to clear the air between us. Nothing is going to stand in our way, gypsy." His smile was as beatific as Mrs. Baker's.

He helped her to the car as if she were some precious

package, putting her in and fastening her seat belt securely across her chest. "Lucky your wound is on the other side," he commented.

"Oh, yeah, lucky," she said sarcastically, feeling helpless against his take-charge attitude. "Reid, there's not going to be anything at all between us. Is that clear?"

He leaned over her, his hand slipping around her waist, his head dipping toward hers. If he had used force, she would have resisted the kiss, but his technique was persuasion and cooperation, freely given.

His lips were warm and seeking, searching for some hint, however slight, of the passion that had once burned so brightly between them. He subtly explored her mouth for forgiveness of the youthful hurt he had inflicted on her.

She tried to withhold herself from the kiss and from her own emotions, willing herself to remain passive. It was like trying to hold back the wind. Futile.

Catching her bottom lip with his teeth, he held it captive while his tongue brushed back and forth with rapid, feather-light strokes that fanned the embers from so long ago. Embers that had never died, she acknowledged painfully.

"Such sweet torture," he spoke against her lips, his slight beard rasping against her chin. His chest moved in a deep breath. His lips set a trail of fire as he moved to her neck, pressing his face there to inhale her scent.

"You smell of flowers and Christmas spices and piny woods. All the good things in life. We'll find them all again. We'll have it all," he whispered fervently in a promise to both of them that seemed born of some inner desperation of his own.

Keri experienced the emotional pull of that promise

and was forced to concede that it was more than the bayou country she had missed during her ten years in Texas. "We had better go," she murmured. She felt as fragile as a piece of tissue paper, ready to tear and shred at the slightest touch.

"After we made love . . ." He raised his head to gaze into her panicky countenance. "After we made love, we would lie in the dark and talk. For hours and hours. About everything. The world. Politics. Education. I've missed having you to talk to."

Keri leaned her head back on his encircling arm and stared into his darkened eyes. She was helpless before the tortured memories she saw there. "You had friends," she reminded him. "A town full of them. The men you grew up with . . ."

"That wasn't the same. Two men can't share what we had," he told her, his fingers kneading into her side to convince her of his truth. "Our thoughts, even when we disagreed, meshed perfectly. We were *close,* mentally as well as physically."

Gently caressing her breast, his hand leisurely moved to her thigh, bringing fire to the flesh through the light material of her slacks. He rubbed seductively from the groove of her hip to her knee several times while his lips kissed her closed eyes, her temples, her forehead.

With only the very tips of his fingers, he gently stroked along the inner edge of her legs at the point where they met.

"It's all right," he soothed her tensing actions.

The tender assault continued until, against her will, her body relaxed under the hypnotic massage. His touch seemed to convey a message her mind didn't comprehend.

When he raised his head, she opened slumbrous eyes to stare at him from confused depths.

GYPSY ENCHANTMENT

"Have you found what we had with anyone else during all these years?" he demanded huskily.

She closed her eyes, turning her face aside.

Strong fingers caught her chin, bringing her back to meet his penetrating search into her past and her soul.

"Yes," she said softly. "With scores of men, with legions. Whole armies have passed through my bedroom." Her face blazed with rising defiance of his seductive tactics.

"I tried to forget when I couldn't find you," he murmured. "First I tried with quantity. When that didn't work, I found a mistress . . . then another. After that, I decided to get married. A wife would make me forget a small female with fire in her dark eyes and passion in her blood, that wild tangle of curls, the tiny dimples that lurk in your cheeks. But all women were insipid—like eating nothing but mush after tasting the feast that was you."

"Surely you exaggerate," she quipped. "Imagination has enhanced your memories. . . ."

He caught a handful of her hair in his left hand. "Was that imagination just now?" he asked with a laugh, his voice going very deep and quiet.

"That was a mistake!"

"Was it?" His thumb arched across her face to caress her reddened lips.

"I just want you to leave me alone. I want to get on with my own life, Reid, not yours." She sounded resolute, but there was a note of despair in her voice.

"I won't leave you alone. We have unfinished business," he stated flatly.

He cranked the engine and, turning the car, once again headed them on the journey to his house. Keri didn't speak and neither did he.

She watched the passing scenery that was so familiar

and yet so new. The woman who had been her first foster mother had lived near here. Granny, everyone had called her.

For some reason, Keri had been a weak baby besides being born six weeks prematurely and weighing less than six pounds. When she failed to gain needed weight, the social worker had arranged for her to live with the older woman, a widow in her fifties. She had stayed with Granny for five years, until the woman had a stroke. Then Keri had been taken to an orphanage. Later that year, Granny had died, and Keri began running away. Eventually, she was labeled as "incorrigible" and transferred to Shreveport.

There were lots of opportunities to sneak away from the orphanage and she had used them all. They would find her walking along the banks of the river or a bayou, her eyes sad as if with unbearable loss, and they would bring her back.

As Reid turned off the highway and headed for the village, Keri wondered what she had been looking for when she went off like that. Had she been trying to find the love and warmth that Granny had given her? Or was it that life had sometimes become too much for her, and she had sought a place to hide until she could face it once again?

Why, after she graduated from high school and was released by the state officials, had she returned to this area? Had she still been trying to recapture the past, find someone to take Granny's place?

She didn't know the answers to those questions, and there was no use in thinking of them now. You can't go back, she reminded herself wearily. You can't ever go back.

Reid speeded up once they were past Beausanville.

GYPSY ENCHANTMENT

Soon he turned at the stone pillars that marked each side of the drive leading to his home. He guided the car up the shaded driveway and parked in front of the steps.

The plantation-type house had a porch all the way across the front, an upstairs balcony and lacy iron railings. She vaguely remembered the large entrance hall, the stairs, and the gallery.

She remembered the impassive butler, too. The man came down the hall from the back of the house.

"Welcome home, sir," he said, reaching for her case that Reid carried.

"This is Miss Thomas, Milton. Do you remember Milton, Keri? He's been with us a number of years." Reid eased them past the awkward introduction and skillfully directed her up the steps with a hand on her arm. She let herself be carried along with the tide.

Upstairs, he led her into a large bedroom from whose windows she could see glimpses of the lake and the levee that bordered the canal along one side of the property. The room had blue walls with dark wainscoting; the furniture was Queen Anne. It was an austere, almost forbidding, room.

"Your clothes are in the closet." At her startled glance, he explained, "I had your secretary pick out some stuff and send it over on the plane. I knew you'd want more than you had in the weekend case you brought."

"Reid . . ."

"You're staying, Keri. At least until your next doctor's appointment. Then we'll talk about it." He glanced around, his sharp gaze making sure his orders had been followed for flowers and fruit to be in the room. "Do you like the room? It was my mother's."

Again Keri had the impression of a small boy offering a gift to someone he wanted to impress. "It's nice," she temporized.

"All right, let's have it. What don't you like about it?" He stalked over to her, placing his hands on his hips as he waited for her answer.

She licked her lips nervously. "It's fine." At his lowering countenance, she added, "I don't care for blue. It's a cold color." She glared defiantly into his frosty blue-green eyes.

He thought for a minute, then, "Come on." Taking her wrist, he pulled her from the room just as Milton appeared at the top of the stairs with her bag and a vase of flowers, plus a basket of fruit swinging on one arm. "We're going to use my grandmother's old rooms," Reid told the surprised man, who quickly composed himself and followed along the hall behind them.

The room was lovely, done in toasty brown tones and shades of buttery gold. An oval rug covered the brown carpet in one area to form a conversation grouping of several small chairs and tables. The rug was woven in a print of autumn leaves; the upholstered pieces picked up the various shades from it. The bedspread and walls were pale gold.

"Well?" Reid demanded.

"I love it. I love it," Keri laughed delightedly. She ran to the windows, which were framed with brown velvet drapes and gold undercurtains. She had a view of sweeping, terraced lawns, dipping from the rise the house sat on, then gradually rising again to the height of the levee.

A door opened into a small room that had probably been a sewing room in another era. It held a desk, several chairs and a couple of bookcases filled with classics.

While she explored, Reid directed Milton—Keri would never have the courage to call the man by his name, it was too presumptuous—to remove her things from the blue room and bring them in here.

The butler said that he would take care of it and have Mrs. Jannis make up the bed in the suite. Reid guided Keri back downstairs where he introduced her to the housekeeper, who seemed more approachable than the formidable Milton. Then they went into the library.

"So many books," she murmured, going over to read some of the titles.

"People had more time to read in the past," Reid commented.

"Instead of watching television, I guess." Keri flitted around, admiring some prints along one wall, of Louisiana scenes. She recognized one of Bourbon Street, thought another was of the fishing boats along Bayou Teche.

"Sit down," Reid commanded, tired of her nervous fluttering. "You're supposed to take it easy," he growled.

She settled like a wary butterfly into a deep chair covered in leather and a muted plaid of blue and green. Over a low side table, she noticed that mounted on the wall was a picture of a woman. It was a full body portrait, about two-thirds lifesize. The woman was Reid's mother. She was tall and slender with light blue eyes and solid white hair that was styled back from her face. Keri had seen her a few times at the restaurant. If you want to meet high society, she silently quipped, be a waitress.

GYPSY ENCHANTMENT

Gazing intently at the face of the portrait, she wondered if Mrs. Beausan had been as cold a person as she looked. For Reid's sake, she hoped not, then threw the tender thought out. What did she care if his mother was a loving person or not?

Her eyes went to the man who stood at the tall French doors with his hands in his pockets. She went over and stood beside him. After a minute, for some reason, she slipped her hand into the crook of his arm.

When he looked at her, she smiled. "You have a lovely home, Reid, lovely and gracious," she said sincerely.

"Thank you, Keri," he responded solemnly.

Milton came in a few minutes later to inform them that the room was ready and to see whether they required his services. Keri shook her head at Reid's inquiring glance.

"We'll want an early tea, after Keri has a nap," he told the butler, who nodded and withdrew. "You need to rest. It's been a long day for you," he thoughtfully explained.

He escorted her to her room where the covers were turned back in preparation for her nap. Reid left her to undress and crawl beneath the clean, sweet-smelling sheets that were the color of butter. She sighed with real weariness, not realizing until that moment just how tired she was. Reid had been right about her needing rest, she admitted sleepily.

Opening her eyes, she stared at the ornate ceiling, noting, for the first time, its elaborate carvings. But her thoughts weren't on decoration.

She wondered about getting away from here, from Reid. Did she really want to? It was still there, the old magic in his arms, the terrible excitement that made her feel almost ill with longing.

Did she want to stir all that up again? And what for? To satisfy his male ego over the "unfinished business"? So that he could be the one to call it off when he grew tired of her?

But she was her own person now. If she wanted to have an affair, she could handle it. With Reid? her common sense inquired. Could she handle an affair with Reid? Could she handle Reid?

Still smiling over this last intriguing question, she fell asleep.

3

At breakfast on Thanksgiving morning, Reid told her of the day's plans.

"Two holiday meals," he said. "One at noon at Aunt Hester's, the other at seven this evening at Aunt Amy's place. In between dinners, I'm bringing you home for an afternoon nap."

"Why don't you have one big meal in the middle of the afternoon here? That way, everyone could come at once, couldn't they?" She propped her elbow on the small round table of the breakfast room and with her chin resting in her palm stared at her host.

She had slept late this morning because they had sat up late last night, catching up on each other's lives in a superficial, hit-the-high-points manner. Both had been reticent in discussing the deeper points or expressing feelings associated with events.

That was just as well, she thought. Keep it light.

Reid finished pulverizing the fried egg on his plate

GYPSY ENCHANTMENT

and stirred the pieces in with a liberal serving of grits. He chewed and swallowed a bite before answering her.

"It's not a matter of everyone coming at once. There's only my two aunts. Neither has children or other family."

"Well?" she asked.

"Aunt Amy doesn't talk to Aunt Hester. That is, not ordinarily. She does if they come face to face in church or at a community function. But they're not friends."

Keri was fascinated. "Why ever not?"

She munched on a piece of buttered toast, which was her usual morning meal, while Reid bit into a huge baking powder biscuit, presumably cooked by the competent Mrs. Jannis. She watched the firm bite of his strong white teeth, then the muscles of his jaw working as he ate. His throat bobbed up then down as he swallowed. He wiped his mouth on a paper napkin.

"They had a falling-out years and years ago."

"How come?" she persisted.

"I'll tell you after we leave. Would you mind if I ate my breakfast while it's hot?" He shot her a teasing look of exasperation.

Smiling, she spread strawberry jam on a toast slice and nibbled silently on it, her attention on Reid.

He forked egg and grits into his mouth, a bit of egg catching on his upper lip. His tongue darted out and brought the erring morsel under control. He patted his lips with the napkin. She remembered him as being a neat, fastidious person in whatever he did.

Over the span of years, they had shared many meals. Those of yesterday and this morning plus all those of long ago. Sometimes she had cooked for him in her one-room apartment with its tiny kitchen tucked into an alcove.

She sighed pensively. The rivets of life. That's what

this sharing of insignificant human acts was. The little bits and pieces that bind lives into a single structure, each part capable of functioning on its own, but, somehow, better together.

Families had these ties of humanness. Husbands and wives. Sisters and brothers. And they throw it away, she acknowledged sadly. As if it were nothing. As if it didn't take years and years to forge those connections, and generation upon generation of human contact. Real, deep, intimate contact.

"Keri?"

Her eyes jerked to Reid.

"I've spoken to you three times," he scolded her for her inattention.

"I'm sorry, I was lost in my mind. It's such a wilderness." She grinned, wrinkling her nose at him in a manner that was engaging and saucy. "What were you saying?"

"How much getting ready do you have to do? I thought we would leave about eleven for Aunt Hester's."

"Could I wash my hair? They only let me take one shower in the hospital. I won't take long," she promised.

He frowned. "I could send Mrs. Jannis up to you if she's still here. She and Milton have the day off . . ."

"Oh, no. That's okay. I can handle it myself. I'm quite capable of a shower and shampoo. I'm not an invalid!"

"I could help," he mused. "But then, we would probably never get to my aunt's." His grin was wicked, his eyes blatantly reminding her of past showers.

An hour later, Keri was dressed, standing in front of a long mirror mounted on the bathroom door. Her dress was a soft knit of deep burnt orange that enhanced her natural coloring, especially the glow in her eyes. She looked as if she were mistress of the gold and brown room, as if it had been decorated with her in mind. Her shoes and purse were brown kid leather; a paisley print scarf was tucked into the neckline of her dress. Her sensuous lips were bright with red orange lipstick and shiny with gloss. Subtle shadings of brown brought out the size and shape of her seductive eyes. She looked fit, her petite figure faithfully outlined by the drape of the knit fabric. No trace of her accident was visible in her sparkling demeanor.

A knock sounded on her door.

"Are you ready?" Reid called through.

"Coming." She traipsed out to join him, slipping her hand through his arm and allowing him to escort her to the waiting car.

She had decided to enjoy this long weekend and return to her home in Houston on Monday. She owed him that much for his companionship and help during her illness. It was only fair that she reciprocate with her company, since he so obviously desired it—insisted on it.

Once they were on their way, she plunged into the breakfast conversation again. "Tell me about your relatives." Like others who had no close relations of their own, she loved to hear about the families of those who did.

An amused crinkle appeared at the corners of Reid's eyes. He had faint lines in his forehead, too, that hadn't been present ten years ago, she noted.

"Aunt Amy is sixty-four, Aunt Hester is fifty-nine. I think." He considered while Keri waited impatiently. "Anyway, about forty years ago, Amy brought home a new beau. It seems he took one look at Hester and was smitten. . . ."

"How did she react?" Keri asked.

"I'm going to tell you. Don't interrupt." He cocked a warning brow at her, then continued. "Hester thought he was pretty nifty, too. They eloped a week later."

"Poor Amy," she commiserated.

"Yes, she hasn't forgiven her younger sister yet. I guess that was the last chance for her. She didn't marry."

"So what happened to the beau?"

"He and Hester had a happy life in Baton Rouge. He died almost seven years ago—"

Keri looked sad. "And they had no children?" She tugged at the seat belt to loosen it.

"Leave that alone," he commanded, slapping at her fingers. "As I was about to say, they had no children, so Hester moved back to Beausanville about a year after his death. Now she does volunteer work at the school clinic and is on the library board."

"What about Amy? What did she do all these years?" Keri was filled with concern for the one left behind.

"Amy's a lot like you. She opened her own office, and now she wheels and deals in real estate. Farms, commercial sites and offices. She's done quite well for herself. The family fortunes were depleted there for a while. Too much gracious living and not enough attention to the salt mines." He laughed gaily.

She thought about this. "But your father changed all that. He was a huge success, wasn't he?"

The tall, confident man beside her sent her a solemn glance before turning back to the nearly empty street of the village. "Yes, he was a success. He married my mother."

Something about the way he added this last statement stopped the questions that trembled on her tongue from spilling out. She sensed something deeper here and didn't pry.

GYPSY ENCHANTMENT

"I hope Aunt Hester has plenty of turkey. I'm starved," she said.

"You should have eaten a real breakfast," he reminded her with male superiority.

Keri ignored him and continued to admire the neat streets of the town, her eyes drinking in the sights. Huge old oak trees, dripping with Spanish moss, lined the quaint residential street in the area where his relative lived.

A glossy-leaved magnolia had survived the ravages of time and civilization and was featured in a tranquil setting in one yard. The pasture grass was still green in the meadows. The weather was just now starting to cool into autumn.

When they arrived at the neat brick house, Reid turned in, stopping in the paved drive near the brick-lined walk.

At the front door, they were enthusiastically greeted by a tall, vivacious lady who wasn't at all what Keri had expected.

With a name like Hester, Keri had pictured a small, ultrafeminine woman who was kind of sweet and old-fashioned, a woman who would be right at home doing charitable works. Reid introduced her to a modern female dressed in a black pantsuit with a long-sleeved white blouse printed with black plumes.

Her dark hair was mostly gray, and it was cut in a short feathery style that complemented her lively manner. She kissed Keri on each cheek in the European way.

"I'm very happy to meet you, Mrs. . . ." She didn't know the woman's last name.

"Aunt Hester, dear. Or just Hester, if you prefer," Hester said airily, her black jet earrings swinging wildly to and fro beside the oval of her face. "Come into the living room. I have a relish tray prepared. Dinner will be in about an hour if I've gauged the turkey correctly. Is it twenty minutes to the pound? I never can remember."

Waving them into the other room, she continued talking while Reid plumped harem pillows and placed them behind Keri's back in an easy chair. He did the honors with small glasses of sherry for each of them before he, too, sat down to enjoy Hester's prattle.

When she went into the kitchen to check on the meal, Reid grinned at Keri and pulled on his ear as if it were still ringing from the surfeit of conversation.

"Now you know how they got that expression about talking the ear off a mule," he leaned toward Keri to whisper confidingly.

She favored him with a stern frown. "I think she's simply delightful."

"Oh, absolutely," he agreed. "She just talks a lot."

And so she did. The young couple enjoyed a steady spate of local gossip during the delicious meal that had all the traditional fixings, all cooked to perfection.

"No, thank you," Keri said regretfully to another helping of sweet potato pie that was made with pralines and covered with a thick coating of melted marshmallows.

They had coffee in the living room after Reid washed the dishes. He allowed Keri to dry the crystal, china and silverware, but that was all. He sent the two women out of the kitchen while he finished the pots and pans.

Hester got out the picture album and motioned to Keri to sit beside her on the couch. "Here's Reid when Susannah brought him home from the hospital. Wasn't he a doll! We all adored him, naturally. He was the only grandchild."

Keri perused the snapshots. There was a hunger for family reminiscences in her that could never be satisfied, but it was one that she recognized and understood. She enjoyed a vicarious sense of nostalgia and belonging as she listened to Hester's voice.

"Now here's me and Amy and Reid's father when we were still in rompers. Charles was two years younger than me. He would have been fifty-seven now." For a second, her vibrant voice was stilled and a look of sadness crossed her face. "Time seems so short. Amy is five years older," she mused.

"Are these your parents?" Keri asked to distract the older woman's attention. She pointed to a picture.

"Yes. Oh, this one was taken right after Reid was born. Our mother was an Acadian, you know." At Keri's start of surprise, Hester elaborated. "Oh, yes. The daughter of a fisherman. Now, Father was supposed to have married to replenish the family fortunes, but he took one look at this frisky, barefooted urchin and fell in love. Just like Ralston and I did," she said dreamily.

"I see," Keri murmured.

"Did Reid tell you about that?" Hester asked, a shrewd gleam in her eye.

"A little," she admitted.

Hester nodded, her earrings swinging from side to side. "I thought so from the way you've been careful not to ask about Amy and me." She sighed gustily. "It was a long time ago. I wish things had worked out differently. I still love my sister, but she's let this build up inside her. . . ."

As Reid's aunt shrugged helplessly, a flood of sympathy filled Keri. Such a waste of love, she thought, wishing she could do something to help. But it was a problem that only Amy and Hester could solve.

Reid brought in the coffee tray. His sleeves were rolled back on his sinewy forearms from doing the dishes, and his tie was off. Picture of a domesticated rogue, Keri smiled to herself. Barely tamed, she amended as she met his flashing glance. He had that same quality of impatient waiting that she used to see when he came for her at the restaurant, that smoldering awareness of what came later.

A frisson ran down her back.

"Drink up," Reid broke into her mental images. "Keri has to take a nap before we go to Amy's tonight for her dinner," he said easily. Apparently it didn't bother him to speak of one aunt to the other.

"Yes, she mustn't overdo." Hester stood when her nephew did and walked the couple to the door. She kissed them both goodbye affectionately, not pausing in her comments and advice to both of them.

Keri settled gratefully into the comfortable seat. "Ahh, that was nice. Thank you for taking me." She stifled a yawn.

As he pulled onto the deserted street, Reid asked, "Who do you usually spend holidays with? Anybody special?"

"No. Sometimes with my secretary, Marta, and her family."

"Not with your partner?"

"No. I'm buying Mack out. His wife doesn't like me. . . ."

"Jealous?"

"Um-hmm," she admitted reluctantly. "It really aggravates me. Mack is old enough to be my father. We make a good team, but now, well, it's best to go our separate ways."

"How did you get started with him?"

She recognized Reid's delicate probing into her life. Strangely, she didn't really mind, although she would have from anyone else. She wasn't inclined to share her life or herself with anyone.

Nibbling on her lower lip, she reconstructed the past, putting events into order. "Let's see, after I arrived in Houston, I got a job as an inspector in an electronics company. In the evening, I worked as a waitress at a nice family-type place. I took some courses in bookkeeping and found three clients who trusted me to keep their accounts updated. One of them was Mack."

"What did you do in your spare time?" Reid asked in dry tones.

"I studied the stock market and saved my money," she retorted, laughing at the face he made.

"And then?"

"I looked for something to invest in—I had a sizable savings account by then. But I was afraid of the stock market. I had no experience there. Then I thought of Mack's deli. Now food was something I knew about."

She paused while Reid laughed appreciatively at that.

"He had an excellent location in downtown Houston and he did a good business. I knew he could do a lot better. His place needed improving, brightening up. Paint, tables and chairs, that sort of thing. So I approached him with my idea that we would form a partnership. I'd put in new capital while he supplied an established name. I already knew of a location in a shopping mall that we could use to open a second shop. So that's what we did. The rest is history, as they say."

She ended in a breathless rush and met his gaze with a proud one of her own.

With one long, tapering finger, he stroked the slight stubble on his chin. Keri could almost see him thinking through what she had said. "So where does the Silver

Spoon fit in?" he asked. He used both hands to swing the wheel for the turn into the drive at his house. They were home.

"That was a later idea. I incorporated it separately from the partnership. Mack didn't want to go into it with me. Thought it was too risky," she briefly explained.

"Or his wife thought it was too risky."

"Yes," she murmured. She climbed out of the vehicle without waiting for him to come around when he stopped at the porch.

She waited on the steps for him, her mind on the coming problem with Vivian, Mack's troublesome spouse. There were times when she wanted to wring the woman's neck and be done with it.

According to Keri's attorney, Vivian was threatening to sue, saying that Keri had used money from the partnership to start the gourmet takeout business and, therefore, she owed Mack half of that successful operation in order to dissolve the partnership.

The woman was a pest, she concluded as Reid lightly ran up the steps and laid an arm across her shoulders, taking her into the house with him and up the stairs to her bedroom.

"Your aunt told me your grandmother was the daughter of an Acadian fisherman," she commented when they stood outside the door.

Reid reached over and twisted the bronzed knob. "Um-hmm. Gram said the reason she chose the colors for this room was because they reminded her of the sunflowers that grew next to her window at the little cottage where they lived."

His bright gaze flicked over the brown and gold color scheme, and Keri knew that he was seeing his grandmother in it once more. Keri could almost see her, too, flitting around in the quick way she probably had, a tinkling laugh always in her voice.

A hand closed on her shoulder. Reid's face loomed over hers as she looked up. His lips descended on her parted ones, catching her off guard. Her mouth bloomed under his, and her breath was trapped in her lungs. Awareness and longing mingled inside her, making her want to pull his dark head closer, to urge him across the room to the inviting expanse of the bed.

"I'll call you when it's time to get ready for the next feast," he murmured, his eyes devouring her slender figure in a singular look of intense desire. He closed the door between them.

Shakily, Keri slipped out of her dress and shoes. Folding the covers back, she lay down and immediately spun into a daydream of unbelievable rapture that she knew could become very real in just a few moments spent with Reid. However, she wasn't quite ready for things to go that far.

"Neither of your aunts was what I had expected," she said to Reid the next day. It was Friday afternoon and they had walked down to the canal that helped keep the water drained from the wide lawn behind them.

Aunt Amy had been slightly smaller than Hester, but the family resemblance was unmistakable in their oval faces and gray eyes. The older sister was quieter and had a more determined attitude, a stronger personality than the younger.

Keri wondered if the woman would have made a success of marriage. Nowadays, it was recognized, or at least acknowledged, that women had brains and business acumen and deserved a chance to succeed in their own right. But forty years ago, Amy would have been a definite exception. Yet she had made it. The expensive, refined home she had provided for herself proved that.

"You were right. I did identify myself with Amy." Her eyes were cloudy with reflection while she considered the rapport that had developed between her and Reid's aunt.

The two women had the same drive to win out over the odds, to show the world that they could stand on their own two feet without the support of a man to lean on. And they had.

Keri smiled inwardly at the comparisons. However, she could never carry a grudge as far as Amy had in dealing with Hester.

Once having cared for someone, Keri couldn't hurt that person . . . or anyone, for that matter. She had known the sharp stings of life and couldn't inflict others with pain, if possible to prevent it.

Reid caught her swinging hand in his large clasp as they ambled along the high bank. "Yes, in many ways you and Amy are similar. And in many, you're different."

She laughed at him. "That's profound, O great philosopher, really deep stuff. Everything in the world is alike but different!"

Grabbing her other hand, he pulled her to him, holding their hands behind his back so that she had to lean against his chest. Still smiling, she lifted her face to defiantly stare into his aquamarine gaze.

The humor faded at the look he gave back to her. She was stunned by the intensity of his desire. His darkening eyes roamed hungrily over her entrancing features like a starving man admitted to the feast.

"Reid . . ." she breathed in a jerky gasp.

"Don't tease, Keri," he commanded in a deep,

hoarse tone that she had never heard from him in either their past or present association. "Don't be capricious. Don't flirt unless you mean to take the consequences."

Had she been flirting with him? In total honesty, she thought perhaps she had. She had gotten up that morning full of buoyant spirits, a feeling of her own power riding high in her. Why the bubbling joy? Looking into Reid's penetrating gaze, she knew.

Her lips parted slightly, waiting for his touch, suddenly wanting his kiss more than anything in the world. Her acceptance was obvious, registered there in her upturned face for him to read.

Instead of taking what was offered, he smiled at her, causing her eyes to go round with surprise. Dropping one hand, he turned them and proceeded with their walk.

The curving of the shallow canal to the south indicated the end of the Beausan property. The cultivated lawn gave way to a pine woods, thick with tangled undergrowth. They continued walking along the cleared bank.

"There's something I want you to see," Reid said, guiding her along an almost obliterated path that veered away from the canal. In a few minutes, they came to a fence and had to stop.

A house sat inside the fenced yard. A cottage, really, for it was small, no more than four rooms.

"How lovely it is!" she exclaimed softly, the quiet of the woods creating a spell of enchantment about the place as if they had stumbled into a fairy tale.

Flowering bushes dotted the well-tended lawn: hibiscus, gardenia, several large oleanders. A screened back porch made a nice place to sit outside on pleasant nights without being eaten by mosquitoes.

"Whose is it?" she asked.

"Yours," he answered. "I bought it for you."

Her flint-dark eyes took on the opaque depth of the stone. Whatever she thought or felt about this disclosure was securely hidden in the silken smoothness of her lucid gaze.

"I see," she murmured. "When?"

"Ten years ago."

"Before or after your father died?"

"I was looking for a place before. I found this one, but the purchase wasn't completed until after the funeral."

Keri looked back along the path they had followed. She made some rapid mental calculations. Twenty minutes at a fast walk from Reid's home to this cottage in the woods.

Her smile was brittle in its cool control. "How convenient."

She turned and walked quickly back to the levee, the air burning her lungs as it had the afternoon of her accident. Hands curved over her shoulders, gentle in their touch, as Reid stopped her, pulling her reluctant body around so that she faced him.

She raised her head, her expression blandly smooth.

"I'm sorry, Keri," he said simply.

His sincere apology released the frozen anger in her. "How dare you think I would be your kept woman!" she ground out in a low, furious voice. Her throat was raw, seared by each flaming word as she spoke.

"I know," he acknowledged her outrage. "Marriage never occurred to me."

"Heaven forbid! A Beausan marry a waitress? A baby that nobody wanted, a person with no fortune and no name? Don't worry, Reid. I never expected it of you."

She twisted from him and ran along the steep

embankment, past the brick path that wound around flower beds that would have taken her to the main house. She ran to the end of the canal, and there she threw herself to the ground, drawing up her knees against her chest, her arms locked tightly around them, her breath coming in gasps. She stared out at the lake.

Reid caught up with her there. He sat beside her but not touching. She couldn't have borne his touch at that moment. She kept her face averted.

"Do you need a handkerchief?" he asked.

She jerked toward him. "For what? I'm not crying."

"How many tears have you shed in your life?" he mused.

"None. I never cry," she said.

"Never?" His gaze was so soft, as soft as summer sunlight.

"Never," she swore. "But if I do—and I'm not saying I ever have—I'll cry alone . . . and in the rain."

"I've cried," he confessed, "for you and for me."

After that the silence between them grew and, as the warm breeze from the lake eddied around their bodies, gradually the tension lessened.

When the curve of her spine relaxed into a natural posture, Reid began to question her on her life. "Weren't you tempted at all, these past ten years, to marry? Didn't you meet anyone you considered as a husband?" he asked.

"No. Maybe one," she finally admitted under his continued probing, "but he was already married. What about you?"

"I told you about that the day I brought you home from the hospital. Do you want another demonstration?" He moved closer.

She inched away. "Forget the feast-and-famine analogy. Weren't you tempted to marry for expediency? To produce an heir for the empire? Your father . . ." She halted her words abruptly, realizing too late where her tongue was leading.

"So you realized that, did you?" Reid didn't seem upset that she thought his father had married the Texas heiress for her money. "We Beausan men are sometimes slow to see the treasure hidden right under our noses, but eventually, we catch on."

He reached out a lazy arm and pulled her against him so that she leaned into his chest. He wrapped both arms around her slender form, lacing his fingers together over her tummy. His chin brushed her hair as he talked.

"Back before 1930, the biggest oilfield in Texas was Spindle-top on the Gulf Coast. It was controlled by the northeastern oil companies, the robber barons, who forced out the small guys. Then, late in 1930, the East Texas pool was discovered—*poor-boyed* was the term, meaning the first successful well was drilled on credit by some wildcatter working on his own."

Keri laid her head on Reid's shoulder in order to look at him as he told his story. He dropped a kiss on her nose.

"The big boys ignored the find. Their geologists said there were only isolated pools in the area, not worth bothering with. They were in for a shock! The second well came in about thirteen miles north of that and another twelve miles north of the second."

Reid laughed his deep, masculine chuckle, and Keri grinned in anticipation of the ending of the tale.

"All three wells were from the same pool, and the little guys were buying up oil leases right and left, borrowing every penny they could get. My mother's grandfather was one of those independent drillers."

"Oh, that's how he made his money!" Keri caught on to the purpose of the recital.

"Right. When my mother and father met, both families pushed the connection. Mother had money inherited from her grandfather; my father had an old name and extensive holdings but needed new money to refurbish and stay in business. So, I guess you could say it was a partnership, like you and Mack formed, but with bedroom privileges.

"My mother was a quiet woman," Reid continued. "It wasn't until she had a couple of miscarriages and a stillbirth that the doctor told my father there mustn't be any more pregnancies. As luck or fate would have it, she conceived again."

"What happened?" Keri asked when he was silent a moment.

"Oh, the usual. She miscarried, nearly died. When my father realized what was happening, it woke him up to the fact that he wanted his Susannah more than anything in the world. I was six or seven at the time, and our house became a wonderful place to live in after that. Of course, it was years before I realized why."

Keri pictured the flowering of love in the big house set in its lovely gardens. "Yes, I understand."

She suddenly understood the portrait in the library. Reid's mother wasn't one to expose her emotions to the world. Like herself, Susannah Beausan had clothed her deepest feelings in outward composure. Only to Charles, the belated husband, and to Reid, the happy child, had she expressed her love.

"I'm glad that it worked out for them," she murmured.

His arms tightened around her. "So am I. But now let's concentrate on us. When I couldn't find you, I knew what I had lost. I want it again." His voice was deep, seductive.

"How many mistresses have you had in the little

cottage in the woods, Reid?" she asked with deliberate cruelty.

He winced as she meant him to. "A couple," he admitted. "I told you that before. But it was no good. Life was no good without you."

With brisk movements, she stood, slipping out of his arms like a wisp of smoke. "You managed to survive okay."

His fascinating gaze sparkled over her. "It was only survival, not living. I intend to live from now on. With you," he said to her retreating back.

4

"Well, it's back to the mills and salt mines for me," Reid announced Monday morning over his second cup of coffee. The quip was an old joke between Keri and him, literally true, since an extensive salt mine was part of his business empire.

"You can use the desk and phone in the library. I'm sure you want to check in with your office and your attorney," he continued when she looked up from the newspaper section she was reading.

"Yes. Thank you. I'll reverse the charges. . . ."

He looked pained. "I'm sure I can afford the bill."

"It's a legitimate business expense, tax deductible. And I can afford it, too." Her pride refused to back off in this.

Sighing, he gave in. "Do what you want, then," he groused at her, coming around the table.

He took her arm and pulled the chair back from the table so she could stand up. Placing both arms around her so that he could hold her snuggled to his tall frame, he gazed down at her in a kind of lazy satisfaction. Slowly, he lowered his head, bending a little, curving his body into hers so their lips could meet.

"Ummm," he murmured a few minutes later, "you taste good. Like jam and butter and toast crumbs."

Her fingers skirred through the short hairs at the back of his neck. "You're so romantic, I'm liable to swoon," she whispered with grave melodrama.

He held her off by her shoulders to give her a narrow-eyed scrutiny. "Are you being smart, by any chance?" he demanded.

She very solemnly shook her head in denial. He grabbed one more quick kiss and, taking her hand, made her walk him to the door and stand on the doorstep waving goodbye as he drove off to go to his office at the thread mill.

Back inside, she walked down the hall to the kitchen. There she found the butler having coffee and chatting with Mrs. Jannis.

"Uh ... excuse me, Mr. Milton, Mrs. Jannis," she said politely. Looking at the man, she requested, "Would you drive me to the bus station in town, please? I'll be ready in about thirty minutes."

"The, ah, bus station?" he asked, his brows going up so that three arches formed over each one on his forehead.

Keri smiled brightly, confidently. "Yes, the bus station." Before he could ask embarrassing questions, she turned and sped up the stairs to the bedroom. There, she quickly tossed her clothes into her bag, threw the makeup bag and toiletries from the bathroom into her weekend case, and snapped both pieces of luggage closed with a decisive click.

GYPSY ENCHANTMENT

Quickly smoothing her hair into place, she checked her appearance in the mirror. Her cheeks were a little flushed, and her eyes somewhat defiant. Her brown slacks and tan pullover were fine for travel. She would go to the airport in New Orleans and catch a plane for Houston.

Sadness descended like a weight on her slim shoulders and her face blurred for a second. She blinked rapidly.

She and Reid had had a pleasant weekend. On Saturday, he had taken her boating and for a picnic on Lake Pontchartrain. Sunday, they had gone to the little white church in the village where they saw both the aunts. Later, Reid had taken her for a drive after her afternoon nap.

She had directed him to a quiet road near the winding Mississippi. A young couple sat in the yard that she thought had been Granny's. The place looked different, and she was no longer sure that was it.

Turning from the mirror, she regretfully said a silent farewell to the cheerful room. She hated to leave without saying goodbye to Reid, but he had left her no choice.

She carried her luggage down the broad steps to the entrance hall, past the smiling portraits of the gallery. She didn't look at them. Milton came out of the library.

"Mr. Beausan would like to speak to you, Miss Thomas," he said and rapidly disappeared toward the kitchen after waving a hand into the room he had vacated.

Keri stared after the man, then slowly entered the library. Surely Milton hadn't called and told Reid of her plans. She didn't have long to wonder. As soon as she said "Hello," she had an answer.

"Keri," Reid barked at her, "if you leave before I get home tonight, I swear I'll lay an inch of skin off your backside when I catch up with you, so help me God!" He was breathing heavily into the instrument, and his anger smote her in waves through the wire.

"Milton had no business telling you of my plans," she fumed.

"He was following my orders," Reid informed her smugly. "I told him to report every move you made."

"Now listen, Reid Beausan . . ."

"You listen, Keri Thomas! You be there tonight. No more sneaking off like a thief. Do you hear me?"

"How could I not?" she muttered, holding the phone from her smarting ear. He was shouting at her. No telling what the people at the mill thought.

"Keri," he drawled in warning when she didn't accede immediately.

"All right, I'll *see* you tonight!" She plunked the receiver back on the hook with great force. Stalking out of the room, she glared around the empty hallway. Grabbing her cases, she returned them to the bedroom, although she didn't unpack.

Finally, calming down, she went to the library to take care of her business calls. An urn of fresh coffee and a plate of homemade cookies sat on the end of the massive desk. She recognized the apology in the form of a peace offering.

A few minutes later, she was chatting briskly with Marta, her secretary of five years and the nearest person to a best friend that she had.

"Everything is fine with the Silver Spoon shop," Marta reported. "The manager has sent in the receipts of sales, and business is good. Let's see, Paul says everything is okay in the kitchen. Another one of those wine-and-cheese specialty stores wants to stock our bottled sauces, and a restaurant wants to know if we will supply their baked goods."

"We can handle the first, but I'll have to think about the other. We're not a bakery in that sense."

"I'll put them off while you consider," Marta promised.

Keri discussed several more items before concluding the conversation. "Any more on the problem with Vivian?"

"No new developments. She hasn't filed a suit yet. Vic has your number there in case he needs to call you. Honestly, that woman is off her rocker! Why don't you tell Mack—"

"No!" Keri cut off the words before they were spoken. "I won't tell Mack anything. He loves her."

Marta sniffed loudly. "Yes, but the irony of accusing you of stealing when she had been dipping into the till . . ."

"Marta!" Keri reprimanded her secretary sharply. "Enough said. I plan on coming home soon. I don't know exactly what day, but I'll keep in touch. Call me at once if you need me."

"Okay, boss. You just take it easy and concentrate on getting well. Between me and Vic, we can handle this end."

Keri debated on calling Vic Zimmerman, the attorney who had advised her on all legal work since she had gone into business with Mack, first setting up the partnership, later advising her on starting her own company. He was a good friend. Too good, she admitted, the only man to tempt her since Reid.

Keri had been one of Vic's first customers when the young lawyer was struggling to establish a clientele.

They had labored together, working out the legalities of state and local licensing rules, figuring out clauses in leases and deciding on the best bookkeeping practices.

One night, finished with the grueling task of wading through some government regulations, they had accidentally brushed shoulders while leaning over the desk in his office. Their eyes had met, locked . . . But Keri had broken the eye contact. "I need a friend, Vic, not a lover," she had said. "I'm not a homewrecker; you're not a philanderer."

The moment had passed and not come up again. Now Vic and his wife Nell had a house in the suburbs where she visited occasionally for a cookout. They usually invited an extra man along for her. Like all the married women Keri knew, Nell was intent on marrying her off. Keri wasn't sure if that was because they were concerned with her happiness or if it was a way of trying to protect their own territory.

Several expressions chased over Keri's face: amusement, irony, then a stillness as she wondered why Reid hadn't married. Sighing, she picked up the telephone and dialed the number of her attorney in Texas.

Keri was in the library when Reid came home at six that night. Her nerves were frazzled from all the planning she had done during the afternoon, the arguments she was going to use on him if he refused to let her go, the scathing words she was going to say that would flay him alive!

His smile was perfectly urbane when he swept in, tossing a briefcase onto the desk, then coming over to her. Placing his hands on either arm of her chair, he stooped over to claim a kiss as his right, and rebelliously, Keri turned her head away to avoid his lips.

Reid drew one sharp breath then gritted, "Don't play games with me, Keri. I'm in no mood for them."

One artistic finger touched lightly under her averted chin; using only the slightest pressure, he lifted her face to his. His lips covered her mouth in his usual kiss of sensual expertise, making her want more from him, much more.

But there wasn't going to be more, she reminded herself sternly. This time it was going to stop right here and now. Reid Beausan had to learn he couldn't have it all his way.

"What?" she asked, realizing he was talking to her.

"I said: How was your day?" He quirked one brow at her. "Did you get your affairs . . . your *business* affairs straightened out?"

"Oh. Yes. Everything is under control," she said.

Where were all the brilliant, logical arguments she had formulated that afternoon? She couldn't seem to muster up one to support her contention that she needed to leave right away.

"Reid," she began tentatively.

He walked over to the liquor cabinet, extracted a small glass and poured her a sherry. "Here, darling. You seem nervous," he purred as he handed it to her. "You should calm down before we have dinner, bad for the digestion, you know." He was all concern!

She accepted the glass, started to speak while she had his attention, but the words wouldn't come. He strolled over and prepared a small drink for himself. "You needn't be scared," he continued, his voice as smooth as the murmur of the sea at low tide. "I'm not going to beat you. That was only if I had to come find you."

Anger began to heat her blood, then Reid pivoted his

head, his fantastic eyes holding her in his look. She recognized the quality of impatient waiting, that leashed passion that could explode into tenderness or cruelty in a flash at the right provocation.

In the past, she had only known passionate tenderness from him, but now? There was a hunger of ten years' duration in him; perhaps it would be best to appease that before she broached the subject of going home. Who did she think she was kidding? her common sense chided. Whose hunger needed satisfying?

The tiny dimples appeared in each cheek, but they weren't the result of a smile. Her mouth contracted in fury at herself and her own weak emotions. She wasn't going to give in!

"How was your day?" she asked coolly, poise and determination evident in the question.

"Are you really interested? Or are you trying to divert me from my ultimate goal? It won't work," he stated flatly.

"Goal?" She arched her fine brows disdainfully.

"You know. I don't have to put it into words." Suddenly he was standing beside her. His hand reached down to her. "Or do I? Do you want to hear me say how much I want you?"

He sat on the arm of the chair, his weight causing a slight squeak of protest from the wood. His fingers tangled in the cloud of tumbling curls that hung past her shoulders.

"Is that what you want, gypsy?" he crooned, his voice soft with restrained menace.

A shiver chased along her spine as she stared up at him, her fingers clutching the small glass that was no protection at all.

His lips curved into a sardonic smile. "I don't mind

GYPSY ENCHANTMENT

admitting my feelings. I want you. I've lain awake nights dreaming of making love to you again. No other woman has ever satisfied me since you." He bent to speak close to her ear. "Does it please you to have so much power over me?"

Keri shook her head dumbly, unable to speak. His regard of her was a scintillating experience, making her glow someplace inside. Deep within her womanhood, a fire was starting and every word, every glance, every action of his fueled that fire. She knew how it could rage out of control.

There was a soft knock on the door. "Dinner," Milton called politely from the hall.

Reid released her hair, and Keri found she could breathe once more as he moved to let her up. Rising, she accepted his hand as he escorted her to the dining room.

The meal was a strained affair as the butler moved about on cat-quiet feet, serving salad, a chicken-and-rice dish, vegetables and finally dessert. Keri refused the latter with a curt, "No, thank you, Milton. I've had enough." She had no trouble with his name this time, and her volcanic eyes were frankly accusing as she glared at him. A dull flush spread up his neck.

"Stop harassing Milton. He was doing his job," Reid ordered in a lordly manner.

"Nobody likes a tattletale," she muttered caustically. Her lips formed a pout of irritation.

Reid's mouth twitched with a smile, and he hid behind his cup, sipping the hot coffee while his eyes renewed their smoldering contemplation of his guest. At last, he stood, signaling the end of the dinner, and they returned to the library.

Keri was aware of Reid's slightest change in mood.

She had seen his amusement and the return of the leashed patience. She knew that time was running out.

She glanced at him as he settled on the extra-large, heavily padded sofa opposite the chair where she perched uneasily. She looked away. There was no mistaking it—he was making love to her with his eyes. One by one, he was stripping the clothes from her body, his memory supplying details as he moved over each enticing spot.

"Keri," he murmured. "Come here."

She clutched the arm of the chair. "Really, how was your day? Everything okay at the mines?" she asked desperately.

He sighed loudly. "There's some leakage, salt water intrusion at one of the sites. We're not sure where it's coming from. The engineers are studying the problem. In the meantime, we've evacuated that chamber and the adjoining ones. I don't want to take any chances with the men."

"Oh, yes. I mean, of course not."

Silence. Then Reid kicked off his shoes, stretched out with his head resting on the pillowed arm of the couch. He held out a hand.

"Come here," he coaxed in a throaty voice.

"No." She closed her eyes against his allure. That strong masculine body lying there, waiting for her to join him, each knowing the ecstasy they would find in the other—it wasn't fair of him to tempt her this way. "I want to go home. To Houston."

"You said you would stay until your doctor's appointment. That's not until Friday."

Focusing her dark gaze on him, she denied his words. "You said that. I didn't agree to it."

"You didn't disagree," he told her.

"You make me so angry," she ground out between clenched teeth.

"That's not half what you do to me!"

With a sudden lunge, he was off the sofa and beside her, scooping her into his arms and, before she knew what he was doing, striding out of the room like some kind of conqueror.

Milton was in the hall as Reid started up the broad steps. "Would you care for coffee in the library, sir?" the butler asked.

"No," Reid replied calmly. "That will be all for the night, Milton."

"Thank you, sir,"

"You, you beast!" Keri spluttered. "You can't do this," she protested as he kicked open the door to his bedroom and with the same forceful motion, closed it behind them. He put her down on her feet beside the king-sized bed.

"You belong to me." His aquamarine eyes flowed over her possessively. "I had meant to wait until after you saw the doctor. I was going to take you out to dinner Friday night, then bring you back here. But I think you need to be shown that you are very definitely mine."

"I am not a possession! You don't own me. No one ever has or ever will." She backed from him, came up short against the bed.

He shook his dark head. "It works both ways, sweetheart. Whether you want to admit it or not, we belong to each other."

His long, slender fingers closed over her shoulders with the delicate touch of an artist working clay. He molded his hands to her form, kneading her soft flesh. For several tense seconds, she stared into his devouring gaze, watching the patient quality that had been there earlier be replaced by his unleashed desire. "Come to me, sweet gypsy," he murmured, beguiling her with his longing as he stroked her body.

His hands slipped along her back, bringing her inexorably to him. He moved forward, one foot sliding between her feet, his thigh pressing against hers. "Come to me and make me live again," he whispered hoarsely as his lips came down on hers.

He stole the very air from her lungs; she went giddy with the boldness of his attack. His mouth, hot and plunging, plundered the intimate cavern of her mouth until she was desperate. Retreat was no longer possible, argument was useless as her scant defenses buckled and collapsed.

She wanted him, had wanted him from the moment she'd opened her eyes that stormy night and looked into his. Even then, her first thought had been of him as a lover, although she had tried to deny him that right. But now, she could no longer deny anything. She wanted him!

Of their own volition, her arms wound around his broad shoulders, circling him with her warmth. When he released her lips to explore her throat, she rained kisses along his cheek as if she really was trying to inject her life force into his.

"Oh, Reid," she cried on a soft moan of rapture.

"It's going to be so good," he groaned deeply, his teeth nipping along the ridge of her neck, stirring her passion.

His hands strayed along her spine, down into the small of her back, back up, sliding under her tan pullover to caress the bare skin along her sides. He found her bra strap, and disposed of it with a minimum of fumbling. Spreading his hands broadly across her, he pulled her into closer contact, making her aware that his male desire was a physical thing, not just a vivid memory.

The sinewy strength of his muscular frame became rock-hard in response to her own overtures as she arched her body into his. Her hands set off fireworks wherever she touched, and she was truly cognizant of the power she had over him. It gave her a heady feeling—to know that she could arouse him beyond his iron control.

Reid had removed his coat and tie when he came home. Now Keri pulled and tugged at his white shirt until it was free of his suit pants. Then her hands were on his flesh.

Reid buried his face in her hair. "Sweetheart, sweetheart," he breathed against her neck, causing chills to race all the way to her toes.

The fire was blazing higher in her, and she clutched him fiercely to her. Her fingers found the buttons on his shirt. One by one she unfastened them while his eyes seared her. She pushed the shirt off his shoulders and down his arms until it dropped to the carpet at their feet.

Before she could start on his belt, he interceded. "You next." His deep voice rolled over her in crashing waves. He stripped her sweater over her head in one smooth motion, taking her loosened bra with it.

Immediately, his hands cupped her breasts, bringing them upward for his heated inspection. Her nipples contracted wantonly. He laughed in anticipation, then bent to taste the tempting morsels, kissing the hard tips until little shoots of excitement made her whole body tremble.

"Reid, don't! I, I don't think I can stand it," she

pleaded. It had been so long since she had known desire in this man's arms. She thought she was drowning, perishing in a sea of bliss.

"It's good, isn't it?" he demanded, raising his head. "Say it's good!"

"Oh, yes. Unbearably good," she whispered. Her hands returned to her self-appointed task of undressing him.

He let her proceed until he stood naked before her, proudly male and unembarrassed by his body's natural reactions. Lazily, he reached for the button and zipper of her slacks. In another minute, she stood nude, too.

Smiling, Reid once more clasped her shoulders, nudging her backward to the luxurious quilted bedspread.

"For a man," he said, "everything is so up-front. But a woman—she's a secretive creature, small, demure, her passion hidden in a thousand tiny crevices that a man must find." He drew a shaky breath into his lungs. "I remember all of yours, darling," he concluded.

Laying her down, he pressed her deeply into the mattress, covering her with his body. Then he demonstrated that he did indeed remember all the secret channels of her desire.

Propped on one arm, a leg wrapped securely over her as if to prevent her escape—as if she were capable of running away at this moment!—Reid plied her with kisses and long, stroking caresses that became more and more intimate and insistent. He thoroughly explored every square inch of her skin before he went on to the next. His lips dropped kisses wherever they would fall. On her breasts, across the smooth flat expanse of her abdomen, along her thighs until they found the inward route of her awakening.

GYPSY ENCHANTMENT

"Oh, Reid," she gasped in uncontrollable need. With unexpected strength, she pushed him over, rising to cover his chest with her own kisses. Now it was she who explored, she who rediscovered all the exciting areas of touch that he liked.

With silken motions, she followed the contours of his ribs, trailed languid fingers down his sides, along his hips and thighs. Her lips sucked gently until his nipples contracted into tiny pebbles. She smiled into his eyes while he watched her hungrily. With her tongue, she probed into the shallow circle of his navel, eliciting a low groan of excitement from him. His hand explored along her hips, fingers curving into the softness of her bottom.

His body was familiar to her in so many ways: she remembered the feel of him as her fingers tenderly touched the keys to his passion; she recalled the taste of him as she nibbled at his masculine form; and she reexperienced the smell of him as she sniffed the aftershave along his strong, slightly raspy jawline, the spicy deodorant of his underarms, and the faint, lusty scent of his maleness.

"No, baby, that's enough," he gasped thickly when she became especially bold with her mouth and hands. He pulled her to his chest, twining his legs with hers.

Their mouths met in long, drugging kisses while fires raged between them.

"Haven't you missed this?" he demanded huskily, his hand sliding between them to cup her breast. "And this." With a sudden twist that caused the room to swirl, he turned her until he was once again in the superior position. He massaged a path to her thigh and then stroked the little kernel of desire until she was at the exploding point.

Urgent cries burst from her throat, but he refused to

heed her gasping demands. Deliberately, he provoked her with movements of his body against hers as he arched between her thighs, together but not quite one.

"Didn't you?" he murmured against her lips.

"Yes, yes, I missed it. I missed you," she confessed. She pulled him fiercely to her. "Please, Reid, please, don't tease. You told me not to. Don't you, either."

"All right, darling. I'll give you what you want, what we both want," he promised in a heated avowal.

She felt the controlled thrust of his body crowding her into the covers beneath them. Then he was still.

"Don't move," he warned.

But she was beyond waiting. "I can't help it," she panted. Her body writhed, demanding his participation in the exquisite firing of her passion. She was heading for the starburst, completely caught up in the destruction of her senses that was rapidly approaching.

"Gypsy!"

Reid was with her as one when it happened. Together they experienced a cataclysmic explosion of the known universe that swept them both away on an endless, heavenly journey.

She had told him that she was just a recreation, a thing to be played with at his will. She had been wrong. Together, they were a re-creation of life, a reaffirmation of the creative forces of nature. They were man and woman, combined into one perfect whole being.

The shock waves continued to ripple through their tightly clasped bodies for long minutes after the starburst receded, leaving them too weak to move. They were defenseless in the aftermath, open to the world and to each other. Eventually, Reid rolled to his side, taking her with him.

Still later, when they were both breathing normally again, he spoke. "How could you leave this behind?"

GYPSY ENCHANTMENT

Keri tasted the sweat on his chest with a lazy tongue. She didn't answer his question.

"I realize that you were hurt when I told you to go home, that I didn't have time for you right then, but couldn't you have waited? Or at least tried to contact me?"

She heard the note of hurt wonder in his voice and was helpless before it. "I didn't see any future for us then." Unspoken but heard by both of them was the rest of her thought: "Or now." She tilted her head in order to look at him.

His eyes still glowed with the passion whose embers had never gone out between them. He smoothed the wild tangle of hair from her damp forehead. "We'll work it out. We'll have it all again, just as we did all those years ago and as we did just now."

But Keri knew that the past was gone, that it was an illusion to think one could recapture a thing once spent. Time, like money, could only buy the moment, not forever.

"Was it ever like this with your Texas lovers?" Reid asked suddenly, jealousy rampant in his piercing look.

"No," she said sleepily. Texas lovers! She'd been working at least three jobs most of her time there and she'd hardly had time to eat and sleep.

"Not even the one you liked?"

"I told you he was married. We didn't even share a kiss. Not one."

Reid relaxed beside her. "I'm sorry. I'm just so damned jealous of everyone who shared those years with you, even your secretary that I talked to while you were in the hospital. She knew all about you and I didn't!"

"They only know me in a business sense." She soothed him as best she could.

GYPSY ENCHANTMENT

"Don't leave me again, gypsy." It wasn't a request but an order.

"Reid, we need to talk . . ."

"Shhh," he whispered. "Later. I promise." He yawned, making a purring sound deep in his chest. Then he settled her more comfortably against him and drifted into sleep.

Keri was wide awake. She surveyed the master suite. The room was furnished with a designer's sense of color, using gray, blue and yellow. There was a gray carpet; the wallpaper was a muted blue and gray design, the furniture was covered in misty blue velvet, and bright splashes of yellow were caught in an oil painting of a summer garden, a lamp base and matching ashtray, and in a pile of yellow, gray and blue cushions on the settee at the end of the bed.

Her gaze strayed to the man who slumbered so securely in her arms. She understood him so much better now. It was obvious that he was reaching back to a happier time in his past through her and their association. He was trying to recall the time when he was a young man on top of the world, when his parents had been alive and he didn't have the responsibility of the Beausan empire resting solely on his shoulders.

Certainly, she understood that very human desire. She smiled tenderly at him. Reid was very, very human. Passionate, jealous, demanding, possessive. All of those. And she loved him with all her heart. But she realized that they couldn't return to the early days of their romance. She had finally learned this lesson after all the years of running away.

She knew now that the reason she had come to this area after she was free of the orphanage officials was that she had been happy here with Granny, and she had wanted to find that happiness again. Of course it

GYPSY ENCHANTMENT

had been impossible. Granny was gone; the child, Keri, was gone. The house belonged to someone else. Life moves on, she thought. People have to, too.

She stared at the ornate ceiling with its blue and white carvings. She appreciated the artwork with a small part of her mind, but most of her thoughts remained with Reid.

What should she do? Stay until he woke up to the facts of life? Until he grew tired of her? Could she take it?

Each time they made love, it would be a new link in the chain of life, binding her closer to him. Next to love, passion was the strongest tie between a man and a woman, she thought. And she was tied with both of them, love and passion. They were such tenuous bindings and yet so strong. They could withstand all kinds of catastrophes, yet be shattered with a word.

She went to sleep at last, only to waken sometime after midnight. Reid's arms were cradled around her, his lips on her breasts. His passion kindled her desire to matching heights, and she knew again the wonder of the universe in his embrace.

Take the present, her common sense advised. Let the past and the future take care of themselves.

"Yes," she whispered, "yes."

5

"Mmmm." A low moan was forced from Keri as she woke the next morning. She moved carefully, finding a soreness in muscles she had forgotten she had. Her left shoulder, the injured one, especially protested any movement.

Opening her eyes, she encountered Reid's amused glance.

He bent his dark head over her, the lemon scent of his shampoo filling her nostrils as he tenderly kissed all along her aching limbs, then down to the funny-shaped scar halfway between her shoulder and her breast.

"I'm sorry if I hurt you," he apologized. "I seem to be saying that to you regularly these days." His brow furrowed in concern. "Are you okay? Did I hurt you?" he asked anxiously.

Her fingers combed through his soft hair, loving the feel of it. "I'm stiff," she admitted, "but not hurt. I only remember ecstasy," she said, knowing what he needed to hear.

He looked relieved, then his long lashes dropped over his eyes in a seductive look. "Didn't I tell you how great it was going to be?"

She laughed out loud at him. "Yes," she replied as his arms tightened around her. "It was great."

His lips continued on a path to the tip of her breast. "I'm going to give you breakfast in bed," he whispered. His mouth closed over the pink areola, his tongue bringing pleasurable sensation to her entire body.

"That's lovely, but couldn't we have something a little more substantial than lovemaking?"

His laughter was a delight, throwing open the new day to untold joy. "This is only an appetizer. I meant I was going to bring you a real breakfast, food and everything." Still laughing, he tossed the covers off and swung his legs over the side of the bed.

Keri turned on her side and curled her body toward his. She ran her fingertips through the sprinkling of short, silky hairs at the small of his back, then over to trace the slightly puckered scar from the fishing knife along his hip.

"I love your body. It's so strong and handsome," she murmured. "You give me such pleasure."

Before the admission was completely out of her mouth, his hands were sliding under her slender form, pulling her into his arms. "Keep talking like that and you won't get lunch or dinner, either," he threatened. His eyes, as green as the Gulf waters along the sandy shore, washed over her with possessive longing while desire stirred through his lithe body.

He kissed her once, then put her firmly back against her pillow. She watched him slip into a pair of jeans, a little smile playing around his mouth. The room felt empty when he left.

Wincing slightly, she climbed out of their warm bed and, gathering her clothing, dashed naked down the hall to her room. There, she washed her face, combed her hair and slipped into her favorite gown and robe with the bronze lace ruffling around her shoulders. She ran back to Reid's room.

When he returned, he took in her appearance with a knowing smile. She sat propped very prettily among the pillows, waiting like a grand lady for her breakfast to be served.

He didn't disappoint her.

First they each had a grapefruit half. Then, removing a cover from a dish, Reid served scrambled eggs with English muffins. A small glass of milk accompanied her meal. Finally, he poured them each a cup of coffee, laced with real cream, and sweetened with a dollop of honey.

Keri wiped her mouth with her napkin. "That was delicious. If I ever decide to serve breakfast in my shops, would you like the position of chef?"

Reid grinned lazily at her, reached out to flick the lace over her breast. "No," he drawled, "I'm satisfied just being your lover."

He removed the tray from across her knees and replaced it with his own strong body. Bracing his arms on either side of her, he placed a number of excruciatingly soft kisses along her jaw and up to her temple, not letting their lips touch as she turned her face to find his mouth with hers. He untied her robe, pulled gently on the gown until her breast came spilling out over the lace.

"I love your nipples," he muttered, his voice going very deep. "Large and luscious." He experimentally tasted the exposed one as if it were a new kind of fruit.

"Like a small scoop of raspberry ice cream on top of a scoop of vanilla."

Keri was sinking under his seductive spell, even when he looked into her eyes with a wicked twinkle in his, indicating he was teasing her. But she knew the seriousness was there, hidden beneath the humor.

With her hands on his lean ribs, she deliberately brushed her thumbs back and forth over his nipples, which rose in excited expectation. She grinned at him as he groaned and plunged his face into the curve of her shoulder.

The playfulness disappeared from him. Quickly now, he stripped out of his jeans, then turned his attention to her. In a second, the gown and robe joined the denims on the floor, and his strong body was pressing hers with thrilling demand.

He took her with him, quickly arousing her to meet his own heated passion. Growling deep in his throat, he devoured her hungrily, giving nourishment to her at the same time.

"Don't you have to go to work?" she gasped, surfacing to gulp in a breath of air before he plundered her lips again.

"Yes. It's early, not even seven. We went to bed at eight last night." He spoke in broken phrases, his lips moving along her face to her ear. He bit daintily on the lobe. Cascades of erotic sensation poured down her neck into her chest.

She held his head to her as he pressed his lips to her throat. Her hands slipped down over his shoulders, along the strong muscles of his back.

"This is what I've missed," he whispered to her. "This. And this. And this." His lips touched her at a different spot each time. "Now I'm alive again. You make me live."

His hands swept down her breasts, over her ribs, her abdomen, all the way down her legs to her small feet.

"You're beautiful, more beautiful than my memories," he said hoarsely.

Touching her thigh, he initiated another flood of desire that caused her to cup her body toward his as he leaned over her. Her fingers caressed the small of his back, then dug into his firm muscles with desperate yearning.

"Yes, bloom for me," he urged, his breath hot against her face as his lips returned to hers, taking the honey from her mouth into his.

Sliding her leg over his hip, she gave herself completely to his bidding. Her nails raked gently along his flesh.

Reid carefully levered his thighs between hers, easing his weight over her, holding himself suspended from her until she opened her eyes and stared into his.

"Take me into you," he whispered, asking her to make the final connection.

Without hesitation, she did as he asked, accepting him willingly, lovingly, as part of her body. The ties of passion tightened about them.

Again that powerful force took over, sweeping them in its path of total oblivion, submerging their individual selves until they were joined into the one whole creation.

Keri poured her soul into Reid, wrapping herself around him, holding nothing back. It was potent and scary; it was love at its most giving.

And when the star burst into a million flaming sparks, she felt she died a little in the explosion. She would never be able to gather all the pieces of herself into one again. Some of her was forever lost to the man who, consumed by his own explosive need of her, surged so brilliantly in her arms.

She held him even tighter as the tidal wave of passion swept over him, leaving him shuddering in her embrace.

When at last he turned, he continued to hold her against his chest as if afraid to let her go, afraid that she might disappear again. His fingers ruffled her damp curls.

A long time later, he said, "There weren't many Texas lovers, were there, darling?" It wasn't really a question.

"No," she answered.

"It doesn't matter," he sighed happily. "There won't be time in your life for anybody but me from now on. I'll see to that," he said confidently, laughing a little.

Her lashes flickered against his chest as she opened her eyes.

"Hey, that tickles!" He rubbed the spot when she lifted her head. He laughed again, a youthful sound. He gave her a boisterous hug, their bodies damp and slippery against each other.

"Reid," she began tentatively.

"I think I could take on ten alligators and whip them," he declared.

Frowning slightly, she pulled herself upright, sitting with her legs crossed beside his reclining form.

He opened one eye, closed it again. "Uh-oh, looks like it's time for serious discussion."

"Yes," she said, refusing to be baited into levity by his mocking tone.

He pushed himself into an upright position against the pillows and composed himself to listen.

"You know this can't last," she told him gently. "I

have my business in Houston to run. Right now, it's going along on its own steam. I have a capable staff, but soon I've got to go back. There are problems coming up that I've got to be there for. You know that."

"Yes, I do." He ran a hand over his face, checking the roughness of his beard absently. "But we can figure it out next week. I have the problem with the salt mine to handle first. Then you have to get your all-clear from the doctor. After that, I'll arrange to take time off to go to your place with you."

Keri was shaking her head when he finished. "That won't work."

His face clouded. "Why not?"

"I can't conduct my life around yours. . . ."

"Can't or won't?"

She glared at his truculent expression. *"Won't,* then! I will not live my life on the fringes of another person's life. I told you that. Everything that I have I've made myself, and I won't give that up!"

Reid smiled suddenly, reaching out a lazy hand to finger one of her curls. "I'm not asking you to give up anything. I don't expect you to neglect your business. We'll just have to work out a schedule so we can be together, that's all. Right now, my business is more pressing, so we stay here. When your affairs demand it, we'll go to Houston. See how simple it is?" His tone was perfectly reasonable, but she knew it wasn't that simple at all.

He left their bed for a second time. "Come join me when you hear the shower running," he said and strode across the room looking as handsome as a god.

Keri sat staring at the spot he had vacated. Hugging her knees to her, she mused pensively on his words. He really was reaching for the past. Sympathy filled her and she was wrung by a tearing sadness. He even looked younger, the years falling away from his face as happiness suffused his countenance. She closed her eyes against the flood of emotion. She should leave while she still could. Each day that they spent together would entwine their lives more.

The longer she stayed, the more tangled their lives became, and the more difficult it would be to leave when the time came.

Yet she couldn't hurt Reid. He was captured by a dream from his past of a happier time. And she knew that the dreams of youth lasted the longest and died the hardest.

The sound of splashing water and a yell from the shower brought her out of her study. Slowly she went to join her lover in the ritual of a bath, another scene from their past.

After Reid had left for his office, Keri, dressed in a pair of jeans and a cotton knit top, wandered down to the library for a consultation with her secretary.

"Marta, this is Keri. Anything new?" she asked after the other woman answered the office phone.

Marta, at twenty-six, was tall, sophisticated, divorced and supremely loyal to her boss. Her blond hair was a cap of tousled curls falling charmingly around her thin face. Her clothes were always fashionable, although not necessarily expensive. Keri knew that Marta admired her—the secretary always said that Keri should be nominated for sainthood.

As she waited for Marta's response to her question, Keri smiled at this idea. She should have seen me in Reid's bed, she thought ruefully.

"Nothing to speak of," Marta hedged. "How are you feeling?"

"Fine," Keri answered, flexing her stiff shoulder to

determine whether this was the truth. She had to admit that the small twinge of pain was nothing compared to the afterglow from lovemaking with Reid. "Wonderful, actually."

"Now that wouldn't have anything to do with the fellow with the deep voice who called a few times while you were in the hospital, would it?" Marta teased. There was nothing subtle about her.

"Maybe," was all that Keri would say, changing the subject abruptly. "Did the truck make the rounds on time today? And have you heard anything on the request for prices from that new guy, the one we were considering as a supplier?"

They settled into a detailed discussion of the business affairs of the gourmet shop. Finally, Keri asked about Mack and the two regular delicatessens she owned jointly with him.

"Nothing new, so far. I've made sure all our books are up to date and in order. Vic said if Vivian filed charges, or talked Mack into it, our records would be subpoenaed. That woman—"

"Okay, okay," Keri interrupted. "Anything else I should know about?"

Silence.

"Let's have it, Marta."

"Well, Chef Paul is threatening to walk out again," she reluctantly admitted.

"What now?" Keri asked. She was glad Marta couldn't see her smile. The chef and the secretary held equally low opinions of each other.

The Silver Spoon kitchen was located in a building of its own, presided over by a Cordon Bleu chef who supervised the turnout of the gourmet foods that were then rushed by special truck to the three shops. In addition to the meats and salads, each store also carried a selection of wines, cheeses and a variety of baked goods also supplied by her gourmet kitchen.

"Oh, you know how temperamental he is," Marta scoffed. "The least little thing sets him off. I don't see why we just don't tell him to go on and leave. Anybody can follow a recipe."

Keri laughed softly. "Yes, that's true. And they could probably produce a uniformly good pâté and custard and vegetable dish. Now when Paul cooks, the results are always excellent, but sometimes . . . sometimes they are more than that, they are superb! That's why we keep Chef Paul."

"Humph!" Marta snorted. "When are you coming home? Or are you?" A worried note crept into the brisk tones.

"Yes, probably over the weekend. I plan to be in the office next Monday. Set up an appointment with Vic, will you? Perhaps a luncheon date. Okay?"

"Sure thing. See you Monday."

They hung up and Keri drifted over to the bookshelves to pick out an interesting novel to occupy her time until Reid came in that night. He had urged her to stay in bed, arrogantly assuming that she needed the time to recuperate from their wild lovemaking during the night and early morning hours. She'd promised to rest after lunch as usual.

"Don't worry, I'll be fresh as a daisy when you get in," she had assured him when he kissed her goodbye at the door.

His heated gaze made her flush with warmth. "See that you are," he had growled.

At six, Keri came down the steps and went into the living room. Spreading the material of her blue pleated skirt smoothly around her, she sat at the piano bench and gingerly touched the keys. Straining her memory, she picked out some major chords, recalled the minors, then played the harmonizing chords: C, F and G.

She loved the sounds of the piano; it had such rich tones, so many voices. She had once taken lessons for a few months. By working in a department store on Saturdays, she had been able to pay for instruction. The foster home where she was living was near the church they attended. The pastor had said that she could practice on the church piano every day after school.

Her fingers faltered over the keys as she remembered why she'd discontinued her practice sessions. One day it was discovered that there was money missing from a Sunday School fund. While the preacher had defended her and insisted that she continue playing there, the joy had gone out of the project, and after another couple of months, she had quit the lessons.

That was one reason why she wanted out of the business with Mack. She couldn't continue to work with him when her every move was viewed with suspicion and she had to defend herself constantly from false accusations by Mack's wife. She would rather sell the deli business to Mack; but he wanted to retire, so she would buy him out.

She was startled from her thoughts when she felt a hard thigh pressed against hers and an arm slipped around her slim waist as Reid sat down beside her. Her face lifted for his kiss even as his hand reached out to bring her to him.

"Hi," he said after a long minute. "You play?"

"No. I always wanted to learn, but . . . Can you play the piano?" she asked, realizing that somebody around here must.

"Some," he admitted. "My mother was very good. Concert pianist material if she hadn't married instead. She tried to push me along those lines. Fortunately, I broke my thumb in seventh grade playing football, and she had to give up that idea, although she made me take lessons for years."

He grimaced comically at Keri. Then with a great show of pushing his sleeves back and flexing his fingers, he struck a resounding chord and proceeded to play magnificently while she stared in wonder, moving over to give him room.

"Mozart," he announced when he finished. His smile faded when he saw Keri's face. "What is it?"

She spoke slowly, as if each word took great effort. "You can play like that . . . you have that kind of talent . . . and you think it fortunate that you broke your thumb?" Her tone was incredulous and angry.

"It takes a certain temperament, too. I don't have that." He shrugged, no apology in his manner, or regrets. "What's wrong? What have I done now?" He was half amused, half irritated with her manner.

"It must be wonderful to have so much going for you that you can throw away a major gift," she said, bitterly.

"Hey, that's not fair." He stroked her hair gently, beginning to realize there was something in her anger that he didn't understand. "It wasn't my fault I was born with long fingers and an aspiring mother. It wasn't in my nature to sit hunched over a keyboard for hours." He tilted his head to one side to study her. "If you want to learn, I'll teach you," he said.

She tried to get up, but he wouldn't let her. Wrapping both arms tightly around her, Reid pressed her head to his chest in a comforting posture.

"No, I don't want to, now. It was a long time ago."

Gently insistent, he wormed the story out of her.

"And they accused you of stealing the money?"

She shook her head. "Not in so many words, but the suspicion was there every time they looked at me. I hated to be thought dishonest. I never took their money!"

"Of course not! Anybody can see you're an honest person." His finger lifted her chin so that he could study her face. "Except you have this disturbing habit of leaving without notice."

"Not without cause!" she protested.

"With me you have to stay and fight our problems out. Understand? No more running away when things get tough."

Milton announced the evening meal. Grinning, Reid went to wash up. He joined her in the dining room a few minutes later and gallantly held her chair and seated her, so full of high spirits that she couldn't help but respond to him, even as she recognized that they were living in a dream that couldn't last. Giving herself up to it, she forgot reality and rejoiced in Reid's company.

The week sped by, each day bringing its own joy. And sorrow, too, Keri admitted on Friday morning as she showered and shampooed her long hair. Each night that she spent in Reid's arms only bound her that much tighter to him. Her love seemed to grow each day until it was a large, aching bundle inside her that only found ease when he was making love to her.

Having rinsed off, she stepped out of the shower and wrapped a towel around her head, turban-fashion. Drying her body, she glanced around the familiar bathroom. All her things were in Reid's rooms now.

Too many ties, she thought, sighing. There were too many rivets bolting her life to his. She had to leave, get out of his house to regain her sense and her perspective.

Love and desire. What silken webs they weave for the unwary. Hadn't she learned anything during her lifetime? Hadn't life taught her not to care too much?

GYPSY ENCHANTMENT

And if she did care, not to let it show? There she was, she continued to harangue herself, giving everything to Reid, telling him everything, letting him see her silly little hurts and pains. She was a fool, an out-and-out fool.

Sitting in an armless rocker, she dried her hair until it fell into its usual deep waves and curling locks. Her dress lay on the bed; it was a soft green silk, for the trip into New Orleans. Reid was coming for her before lunch. They were going to eat in the city, see the doctor for her final checkup, then go out for dinner that night.

Quickly now, she applied deodorant, powder and perfume, then slipped into her pale green underwear. Pulling the green silk over her head, she nimbly zipped it up the back, then stepped into black evening sandals.

She used a smoky green shadow to highlight her eyes, which, next to the tumbling curls that framed her face, were her best feature. Lots of mascara brought out the length of her thick lashes. Powder, blush and coral red lipstick completed her makeup.

The door to the bedroom opened just as she finished transferring the contents of her purse to the smaller evening bag. "Ready?" Reid asked. "The traffic will probably be heavy at this hour." His bright gaze swept over her in appreciation of both her looks and her promptness. "Is it okay to touch?"

"Of course," she responded.

His arms enclosed her lightly, and she let herself rest against him, lifting her face to his and experiencing the never-ending thrill of his kiss. She wouldn't be tired of his kisses even after an infinite number of them, she thought.

"Do I need to wipe my mouth?" He held still for her inspection.

"Yes." She handed him a tissue from her box on the dresser.

He took her arm and hustled her out of the house after removing the signs of their embrace from his lips. He placed her in the car and fastened the seat belt before moving to his side and doing the same. In a minute they were off.

"Our first date," he teased in high good spirits. "I feel like a kid playing hooky with a beautiful girl."

He looked handsome, in a three-piece black business suit. His tie was black with silver chess pieces on it. She knew he kept an electric razor at his office and suspected he had used it before coming for her.

The drive around the lake and into New Orleans didn't take long. It seemed only seconds before they were caught in the lunch-hour traffic which always seemed heavier on Friday than other days.

Reid took her to an elegant French restaurant in the old quarter for lunch. It was awfully dark inside after the brilliance of the noon sun, and he took her arm protectively to guide her to a table reserved for them.

After a salad of marinated artichoke hearts, they had a veal dish with rice pilaf and mixed vegetables. Keri, always on the lookout for new ideas for her lunch boxes, asked for the recipe for the marinade. The waiter obtained it for them, and Reid gave the man a hefty tip when they left.

Keri was pronounced fit after her examination. For a minute, the doctor spoke to her and Reid in his office, cautioning her about colds and fatigue during the coming winter.

"Otherwise, she can resume all normal activities?" Reid asked with such a wealth of meaning in his voice that the doctor flicked an amused glance between the couple before answering.

"Oh, yes," he said, "she can do that anytime she feels up to it."

Keri's face was still red when she and Reid were walking down the hall to the exit a few minutes later. In the car, she frowned at her whistling lover. "Why don't you take out an ad in the paper?—Keri Thomas is sleeping with Reid Beausan," she demanded.

Reid was totally surprised. "What's the matter, honey?" he stopped whistling to ask.

She folded her arms over her chest and refused to answer. Giving her a puzzled glance, he started the engine and drove off, taking her sightseeing along the river then across town along the lake before heading west as twilight gathered the darkness about them.

Keri's embarrassment eventually gave way to a deep contentment as they meandered along some of the older roads instead of taking the interstate highway. Just as she was getting hungry again, Reid turned off the road into a winding drive. Her eyes widened in recognition as he stopped the vehicle in the parking lot.

"Are we having dinner here?" she asked in quiet tones while every part of her cried out to flee. She saw that he was proud of his surprise for her as he nodded.

They entered the foyer of the posh restaurant where she and Reid had first met ten years ago. It was the same place with only a few changes. The color scheme was still red and black with a new carpet on the floor in a red and black abstract design.

Each waitress still wore a short, red dress made like a hunting jacket with a white lace stock and black bow tie. Black net stockings and black shiny boots added the final touches to the sexy outfit.

That Reid still came here frequently and that he had called for a reservation were evident by the greeting of the maitre d', who bowed them to a table next to the window where they could watch the traffic on the river.

After ordering a glass of wine for her and a scotch and soda for himself, he lounged back in his chair, a satisfied smile on his attractive face.

"When first I saw you," he commented nostalgically, "you were leaning over that table right there." He pointed it out. "You turned and smiled, and I remember thinking your smile could stop a raging bull and turn him into a moony-eyed calf, it was so lovely. And still is," he added. "I loved your sense of humor when I got to know you and your willingness to go fishing or hiking through the swamps on a nature trail with me."

Keri found a smile and stuck it on her face. She wouldn't spoil his evening, but she wanted to crawl off someplace and be alone.

"We share a lot of good memories," he told her. The smile he returned to hers had a little quirk in it, a quaint, tender expression.

Oh, Reid, she pleaded, don't you know what you do to me? How will I survive when this is over? What will life hold for me when you're no longer there to woo me with your seductive smile and make me glad to be alive and female?

"I liked you in red. Don't you ever wear it?" he asked.

She shook her head, her hair swirling around her shoulders with a life of its own. "Not since I worked here."

"We'll get you a red dress for Christmas," he began, then stopped as their drinks were served. Reid placed their order without consulting her. He knew her tastes in food.

"A red silk, long and flowing all around you, the way

your hair does," he continued, making it real for her. "You'll wear it to the Christmas party. . . ."

"What Christmas party?"

"I have one at my house every year. It sort of repays my social obligations, celebrates the holiday season and marks another year off my life." He grinned at her.

"Your birthday? You never told me it was near Christmas. When?"

"The twenty-first. There's a lot about each other we don't know, Keri. But we'll discover it gradually." He was serious now, his eyes full of portent as he gazed at her.

So he was looking at a long-range affair, she thought. Why couldn't she just relax and take each day as it came? Maybe their love would last for years. She should try to quit thinking, and start enjoying. Except that she was a long-range planner, too. And she had a life of her own to live, and a business to run.

After a dinner of roast duckling that was as good as any that Chef Paul had made for her, but not better, she and Reid danced to some slow music. Unconsciously, she began to store up memories of her own, enough to last a lifetime.

She noted the things that made him laugh. Sometimes he had a boy's sense of humor, and other times he laughed with the deep, masculine chuckle of a mature male. He had gentleness that was backed by strength and patience, even when she angered him. She treasured the family stories and parts of himself that he had shared with her. All these pieces of him belonged to her, and no one could ever take them away.

"Ready to go?" he murmured later when they returned to their table. The smoldering flames in his aquamarine eyes caused a tremor to start in her.

Instead of driving straight to his house, he turned off

on a dirt road that led through the woods to a clearing beside the canal. He turned off the engine and the lights, and they were enclosed in the cool, soft Louisiana night.

"Remember this place, darling?" His voice was very deep, very husky. "It's where we first made love. Before we realized there was no reason not to go to your place." Laughter strayed over his words. His hands reached for her, lifting her so that he could move over to her side of the seat and hold her in his lap as he had all those years ago.

He kissed her for a long time while his hands roamed her curves with familiar expertise. Keri knew he was remembering that summer of long ago. Inside, she wept.

"Shall we make love here again, for old times' sake? Or do you want to go home?" He was considerate of her tastes and comfort, putting her pleasure first. His lips generated little spirals of electricity along her throat as he waited for her answer.

"Here," she said. She could give him this much, this one night out of the past. A few hours of remembered happiness and that would be it. There was no desire in her now, only a wistful wish to please this man, which she did in the most elemental, satisfying manner, giving in every way that she could.

When they returned to his house, she waited until he was well asleep, then taking her weekend case, she left before the gray of dawn appeared on the horizon.

6

Keri put her hands over her ears until the shrill ringing of the telephone stopped abruptly in mid-ring. She stared at the instrument for a few seconds more before resuming her task.

She mopped the no-wax floor of her kitchen, rinsed the mop and put it back in the utility closet, feeling a sense of satisfaction that the apartment was spick and span once more. In the living room, she straightened up the Sunday paper and placed it on top of the current magazines in their shallow woven basket. The shag carpet, dyed in varying shades of emerald green, had been vacuumed thoroughly, and the contemporary furniture had been polished to a brilliant shine.

She had rearranged the living room. The elaborately carved antique lady's desk that she used at home was in the corner nearest the door to the formal dining room. The green and white brocaded sofa and two green velvet chairs were grouped in new positions off-center to the room. Two old-fashioned platform rockers, made on a small scale, flanked a piecrust table in front of a window.

The green and white color scheme had been used throughout the modern apartment, with its two bedrooms, living room, dining room and kitchen reflecting the colors in various combinations. Except for one indestructible rubber plant, the other pots and vases scattered abundantly through the rooms were filled with dried floral arrangements. Keri could never remember to water her plants, and eventually, all but the rubber plant had died.

After getting a cup of coffee left over from breakfast, she returned to the living room and sat on the sofa, glancing nervously at the silent telephone, half afraid it would start up again as soon as she relaxed. It had been ringing all weekend.

After sneaking out on Reid in the early hours of Saturday morning, the last thing she wanted was to talk to him. She had driven his car to a truckstop on the interstate and called a taxi service to take her to the airport in New Orleans.

Before leaving, she had told the mechanic that the car had a problem and had given him Reid's name and number to call when he got it checked out. On Saturday afternoon, she had phoned the truckstop and found out that the car had been picked up by Mr. Beausan. She had breathed a sigh of relief. Now she could put Louisiana behind her again and get on with her life.

She was running true to form, she thought with a sardonic smile indenting her dimples briefly. Running away when things got too close; hiding until the emotions were suppressed again.

But it was better this way. Reid would soon realize

that he was living in a dream, trying to recapture the past. He was basically too clear-thinking, too mature not to see that. She was simply saving him the trouble of ending their affair. Oh, he would be angry for a while that she had walked out on him again, but he would get over that. He had before.

She was better off here in Houston where there were no memories of the past to haunt her, no person who knew her before she came out here and made a new life for herself. She would forget. . . .

A stabbing pain coursed through her chest, reminding her of the pain of the accident. She set the coffee cup aside and clenched her fists against the tide of longing that made her gasp for breath. Her entire life, from the moment of conception, had been an accident that shouldn't have happened, she raged.

But now that it had, now that she was a living, breathing woman, how could she forget? How did a person forget the ecstasy of loving another completely? How could she forget the heaven of Reid's arms?

Inside her, like a swollen river surging against a weakened dam, the tears threatened her self-control. "I never cry," she whispered. "Never!"

But her heart did. It cried one name over and over, waking her in the dark hours of the night, wanting Reid, only Reid.

And what about Reid? she asked herself. What about his wants and needs, his hurts, the wound to his pride and manhood from this second rejection?

She was torn by the two most basic human emotions —the need to belong, and the fear of being used, of being hurt again if she opened herself to the one she loved.

With a tortured sigh, she paced restlessly around the room. She would always remember Reid's eyes. Each time she looked at the Gulf when she went to the coast, she would see those aquamarine eyes, bold and brilliant as he looked at her.

But she couldn't have stayed! It was destroying her to be with him and yet not have him. His statements about belonging—they were meaningless talk, meant only to win her. Nothing he had done had indicated that he wanted more than her body. And she wouldn't be that, a convenient body, for any man, not even Reid, whom she loved.

She flung herself onto the sofa again and, hugging a pillow to her, stared at the attractive print of green, white and coral. But she wasn't seeing it. She saw only frosty blue mingled with the green of the sea.

"Ohhh," she groaned aloud, in despair.

She could never forget . . . and she didn't want to. Forget Reid? Forget her one and only love? She would have to forget how to breathe first, how to walk, to talk—everything—before she forgot Reid Beausan.

So she would learn to live without him again. All the shattered pieces of her heart ached. She would have to live on memories, forget the dreams. . . . She would have memories. . . .

The next morning, Keri took a cab to work. She made a mental note to see about a rental car until she could replace her Porsche. Something of her old pride asserted itself as she paid off the cabbie and went inside the two-story building that contained the kitchens and the headquarters offices of the Silver Spoon Gourmet shops.

In the neat, rather plain lobby, she went on through to the kitchen to see Chef Paul instead of up the stairs to her office. Paul was gesturing with a wooden spoon and explaining some intricacy of cooking to an assistant when she entered the spotless room, all white tile with stainless steel appliances. With a start, she realized that Paul's strong jawline was very like Reid's, and although he was shorter, his shoulders and general build was very much like her lover's. Forcefully, she put the comparisons out of her mind.

Paul saw her and came forward with a smile. He was a ghetto child from New Jersey, but he had studied his trade in France. Keri considered him an artist.

"We had about given you up for dead," was his opening remark. He took her extended hand and leaned forward to kiss her cheek. His dark eyes surveyed her carefully; then he nodded as if satisfied that she really was okay. "Glad to see you."

"I'm glad to be back. And in one piece," she added with a little laugh. "How are things?"

"Fine," he exclaimed. "No problem."

"I thought Marta said there was a difficulty."

He waved the spoon in the air like a conductor with a baton. Keri couldn't recall seeing Paul without this emblem of his office anytime during the years he had worked here. "It was nothing, a little snooping is all," he assured her, the spoon waving the problem aside. "Your man is taking care of it."

Her man? Oh, Vic must have come by. She wondered what kind of snooping was going on and by whom. She would definitely need to talk to her attorney today.

"Did Marta ask you to prepare lunch? I have a meeting . . ."

"Yes, yes, yes. It is taken care of. Marinated beef julienne with a pasta salad."

"Oh, that reminds me." Keri dug around in her purse while Paul explained the menu he had planned. She found the new recipe, her hand trembling only a little as she handed it over.

"I brought a new marinade recipe we might want to use. Let me know what you think of it," she requested when he stopped talking.

He ran a quick, expert eye over the list of ingredients. His lips twisted thoughtfully while he considered. "It has possibilities. Yes, maybe just a pinch of sweet basil . . . a little more garlic, I think."

Keri smiled as he strolled off, already forgetting her as he considered the recipe for vegetable marinade that she had gotten in the French restaurant in New Orleans on Friday. The color in her eyes deepened as she remembered Friday. It seemed so long ago and was only three days past.

She turned slowly and retraced her steps to the lobby and, this time, went up the steps and into the offices.

Marta jumped up and ran to her as soon as she opened the door. Throwing her arms around Keri, the secretary hugged her as if she had been gone a year rather than four weeks.

"Thank God, you're here!" she exclaimed. "I've been trying to reach you all weekend." She released Keri and went behind her desk, grabbing a tissue and delicately patting her damp eyes.

"What's wrong?" Keri asked, suppressing the pangs of guilt for not answering her phone. It hadn't occurred to her that Marta might have been trying to get hold of her. "Paul said something about someone snooping?"

"That Vivian! She's done it this time. She's got a lawyer representing her, and they've filed suit and gotten a court order to examine all your financial records ever since you went into business with Mack . . . that traitor!" She was up in arms over the turn of events that Keri had been expecting.

"Have you or Vic talked to Mack?"

"No. That spineless worm wouldn't dare . . ." Seeing the look on her boss's face, Marta stopped, but her eyes spoke for her.

Keri heaved a sigh of quiet desperation. "I should have returned last week. Maybe I could have headed this off." She shook her head. "Life gets so complicated."

"I'm glad you're back! Oh, Keri!" Marta stopped. Then, "You have some things on your desk to take care of," she finished cryptically.

"What are they?"

"Oh, the usual, bills and things." Marta was suddenly very casual. It was odd after her initial enthusiasm. "Go on in. The coffee should be ready. Chef Paul sent some cinnamon rolls up. They're on your credenza."

Giving Marta a searching glance, Keri crossed the room to her office, opening the door and walking inside, half expecting to see Vic there. She stopped dead still. The door closed softly behind her.

She clutched a nervous hand on the honey beige material of her suedecloth suit; the other tightened convulsively on the strap of her purse.

Sea bright eyes danced over her trim figure. "Hi, remember me?" Reid asked coolly. A sardonic smile stretched over his lips. He lazily got up from her chair behind her desk and came across the room. "I'm the lover you're always running out on," he reminded her, his eyes narrowing in amusement and menace at her stony stance. He extracted a piece of rope from the pocket of his suit jacket.

Keri's eyes opened wide in alarm. "Reid," she gasped. "What are you doing here?" She squeezed her eyes shut. "Please, go away." She raised her lashes as if expecting him to be gone.

"Rain, rain, go away, come again another day?" he asked in a sing-song voice.

"No, don't come back," she whispered. His face filled her vision, becoming hard with anger as he towered over her small form. Blackness swam before her eyes.

Hands closed on her shoulders. "Oh, no, you don't! You are not going to faint on me. Besides, it won't do you any good. I'll still be here when you come to." Reid pulled her to the chair and pushed her into it. He forced her head down between her knees.

In a minute, her vision cleared. "All right," she mumbled from the thick tumble of hair that fell around her face. "You can let me up."

He released her neck and sat on the corner of the desk. His gaze flickered over her like foxfire, fiery but cool. "What was that little act for?" he asked.

Her eyes went to the rope partially stuffed in his pocket.

"Ah," he drawled, pulling it free again. He held it stretched between his strong hands. "You were right to be scared. I wasn't going to choke you or beat you, though. I'm just going to tie you to me." Smiling grimly, he put the rope away.

Instinctively, she pressed into the chair to elude his fury. "You can't do that!" she protested, afraid that he could.

"Oh, no? Just try me!" He arched one brow. "You're not getting away, not now that I've found you again."

"You didn't find me! It was that stupid accident! You had nothing to do with it!" She felt on the verge of desperation. She didn't want him here. She had no memories of him in Texas to haunt her. Now he would be everywhere in her life, in her present as well as her past. It wasn't fair!

"Fate gave you back to me," he said smugly.

"How did you get here?" A dumb question, as if the answer would change anything.

"Let's see, first in a car, then a plane and then a rental car," he answered seriously. "Thanks for having the *problem* with my car attended to," he added with marked sarcasm. "Why didn't you just ask to be driven to the airport?"

Keri removed her jacket, placed it and her purse in the coat closet, ever conscious of Reid's eyes on her every move. He wouldn't have permitted her to leave the room. Shakily, she poured a cup of coffee and replenished his cup when he held it out to her. She returned to the executive chair.

A hand closed over the fragile bones of her wrist before she could pick up her cup. "I asked you a question!" His anger surfaced from beneath his calm exterior.

"Would you have let me go?" she demanded, feeling a little more in control of herself now that she was getting over the shock of his being there. And, she admitted to herself, she was experiencing a growing pleasure at seeing him, even if he was angry. He had, after all, come after her!

"No," he said in answer to her question. He released her arm and resumed his perch on the desk.

"Well, then, what did you expect me to do?" Her voice climbed a notch in righteous anger.

He tilted his head in an arrogant manner, peering down at her from his greater height. "We could have discussed it. You could have tried using your wiles on me," he suggested.

"I don't operate like that." Her voice was cold.

He walked over to the credenza and helped himself to a sweet roll, holding it in his fingers rather than using the fork on the edge of the dessert plate. He brought her plate to the desk. "Here, you want something to eat?"

Frustration with his high-handed tactics and refusal to listen to her protests made her want to throw the snack in his face. "Reid," she gritted at him, "I don't want you here."

His teasing glance hardened to stone. "Why? Are you ashamed of me?" he growled, sounding like a grizzly on the prowl.

She stared at him, dumbfounded.

"Does it embarrass you for your secretary and staff to know that I'm your lover? Were you, perhaps, planning some clandestine rendezvous, meeting me in secret now and then?"

"I wasn't planning to meet you at all!" she denied.

His eyes narrowed to threatening slits. "Oh, weren't you?" he asked softly. "So you were going to write off what we shared this past week forever. Could you really walk away from that?" His laughter mocked her. "I don't think so."

"You won't give me a chance to find out!"

His hand reached out, smoothing her hair. He leaned over her, his smile wolfish. "You had ten years to find out and it was as if we had never parted the minute you opened your eyes and looked into mine there in the hospital. You knew then that we were still lovers. It was only a matter of time before you were in my bed again."

"I never was in your bed before!"

"All right, your bed, a mere technicality." He dismissed her feeble argument.

Keri was helpless before his inexorable will. He had decided that he wanted her and nothing could change his mind. She could sense the threads of their lives becoming hopelessly tangled.

"You shouldn't be here." Now there was a plea in her voice.

His face softened. "I'm going to help you, honey."

She pulled away from him, reaching to pick up her coffee cup, sipping it to give her time to think. There wasn't one justification that she could think of to get rid of him, other than that he was complicating her life unbearably. He wouldn't listen to that.

"I have people I need to see," she began, thinking of her problems with Vivian.

"If you're thinking of your old Texas lovers, you can forget it! You don't have time for anyone but me in your life from now on, gypsy. No more roaming around, playing the field for you!"

Keri stared in astonishment, realizing that he meant it. He was honestly jealous. "I don't have any Texas lovers, Reid," she said quietly.

"None?"

"Not one."

"Good," he said with supreme satisfaction. "I didn't know how many I would have to fight off."

And suddenly they were both laughing, feeling recklessly gay for the moment.

She arched a coquettish brow at him. "How many women in Louisiana will I have to boot out of the way?"

"None. There haven't been any in a long time, Keri." He chose to answer her seriously. Lifting her in his arms, he took her place in the chair and settled her in his lap.

Before letting her body curve into his, she tried once more to reason with him. Smoothing the dark hair off his forehead, she said softly, "We had a lovely summer romance all those years ago, a delightful fling at a time in your life that was happy and carefree. I can understand that you might want to recapture that time . . . or you think you do. But Reid, the people that we were, are gone. I'm different. You're different. Don't you see that?"

He studied her a long time before answering. "I'm almost thirty-five years old. Well past the age of fantasy. I know what I want. Do you, Keri?"

She looked away in confusion. She had thought she did. Everything had seemed necessary and logical when she had left him. All her reasoning had appeared as absolute truth. But now, with his arms clasped lightly around her, with the hard warmth of his thighs under hers, her thinking went all haywire again.

"Reid . . ."

"Let's try it, sweetheart. Just one day at a time. If it's just a fling, as you say, well, what harm is done? We'll have had a good time together, won't we? Aren't we terrific together?" His breath of laughter stirred a curling tendril at her temple, and he smoothed it into place with his gently caressing hand.

"Yes, but . . ."

"Now," he said briskly, "tell me about this problem Paul and Marta were talking about earlier."

"What about your problem at the mine?" she asked.

"I had to call in a team of experts. My secretary has your number here and at home, so she will keep me informed of their findings. I may have to leave on short notice, but meanwhile, let's see if we can get to work on your little contretemps with your partner."

Leaning into him, Keri told him about it. "Mack isn't the source of conflict, that is, not directly. It's his wife Vivian. She's decided that I used money from the partnership, money that should have been theirs, to start my gourmet kitchen and shop, so she wants part of them."

Sitting up, she glared at him indignantly. "You know what makes me so mad? Before I came along, they were making a comfortable living from their deli, but after we went into business together and followed all my suggestions, their income quadrupled in seven years. That's why Mack can afford to retire now at sixty."

Reid pulled her to him. "I'll need to see your records and the records from the delicatessens, too. We'll plan a strategy with your attorney when he gets here. Do you have your personal bank account records available?"

"Yes." She answered several more questions to give him a clear picture of her business dealings with her partner and on her own.

"You're really something," he said admiringly when she had explained how she got started and her ideas for expanding.

Something warm and wonderful and more than a little scary grew in Keri at his words. She wished that things were different between them, that life had been different. If they were meeting now for the first time, they would be equals and then they could fall in love. . . . But the past was there and couldn't be changed. And while Reid wanted her passionately, he didn't love her. So she would try to do as he asked, live each day as it came, and if life offered chicken one day and only feathers the next, well, that was the way it was.

Vic Zimmerman came at one o'clock for their luncheon meeting. His blond hair and blue eyes didn't stack up against Reid's looks, and she understood what her lover meant when he said all other women were insipid after knowing her. She felt the same.

"Reid, this is my attorney," she introduced Vic, "and

this is Reid Beausan . . . from Louisiana," she concluded lamely, not knowing how to introduce him. Heat suffused her cheeks at the smile that lit Reid's bright eyes at her hesitation. She was also aware of Vic's puzzlement over just where Reid fitted into her life.

"Beausan? I believe I've heard the name," Vic said. His blue gaze shifted from one to the other as his confusion grew.

"My family has some oil holdings in Texas as well as in Louisiana," Reid said easily. "Keri and I go back a long ways. We've been friends since she was a teenager."

Relief was evident in the attorney's face. "Oh, an old family friend. Glad to meet you. Keri hasn't spoken much of her childhood. I've often wondered about her deep, dark past," he teased, flashing her a charming smile.

Reid's large hand slid under her hair to grasp her shoulder in an intimate caress. "Oh, she has her secrets, that's true," he chuckled in his bass tones.

"Shall we get on with lunch and down to business?" Keri reminded the two men who were coolly sizing each other up. She called Marta on the intercom and requested that their lunches be brought up.

A few minutes later, they were seated in a casual circle of chairs with folding trays in front of them. Thin strips of spicy beef nestled at one end of an oval plate which held a cold macaroni salad mixed with pineapple on the other. A smaller oval plate held a medley of steamed vegetables. Hot glazed pears served with fresh gingersnaps was dessert.

Vic lounged back in his chair with a fresh cup of coffee after finishing the meal. "I love lunch meetings with Keri," he announced with satisfaction. "She's my favorite client . . . in more ways than one." His look at her was proprietary.

Reid smiled expansively. He wiped his mouth, crumpled the napkin and tossed it on the empty plate. "Yes, she's special," he agreed companionably. "A woman of many talents." His eyes raked her small figure as if he were totting up her talents at that very moment.

Keri encountered the definitely sexual glance with a small scowl of disapproval. It was unlike Reid to be so obvious. She got up, and after refreshing her coffee, offered a fill-up to the men. Having taken care of that, she removed their trays to Marta's office from where they would be returned to the kitchen.

"Now, what have you found out?" she asked Vic when she had resumed her position.

"Mack, pushed by the lovely Vivian, is going through with it." Vic opened his briefcase and removed some papers, holding them out to Keri.

Reid intercepted the reports, taking them into his capable hands and starting a cursory examination.

A slow flush spread up Vic's face. "Perhaps we had better establish just how much information your friend is privy to," he said in a tight voice.

Keri had scooted her chair near Reid's so that she could peer over his shoulder. Now she glanced up at the tone and realized that he was referring to Reid, who also looked up. His eyes locked with the young lawyer's in a tense battle for dominance.

Keri's dark eyes flashed from one to the other. Why, they were jealous of each other! She was completely taken aback.

Vic was being protective of her. He wasn't only her legal advisor; he was her very good friend. And he wasn't used to her having other men around who were also very close to her. Reid, of course, was being his usual possessive self.

The blue eyes dropped first as the aquamarine ones refused to yield.

"Reid has access to all my records," she said firmly, leaving Vic in no doubt of her trust in the stranger from her past. "Tell me, without all the legal mumbo jumbo, just what Mack and Vivian are trying to do."

Vic explained briefly. "They will go back through your records and try to show you couldn't possibly have invested the amount of money you used to start your businesses from what you had saved. They'll dig out what you spent for food and clothes and for your apartment."

"That's no problem. I hardly spent anything for the first five years that wasn't connected to the delis. I lived very frugally," she declared confidently.

Vic pricked her balloon of assurance. "But they will say differently. Their attorney will try to paint an extravagant picture of luxury living while they had to struggle to make ends meet."

"Well, it's not true!" she said angrily. "You can ask Marta or anybody. The people who worked for me from the beginning know that I put nearly every cent the gourmet shop made back into the business."

Reid patted her arm comfortingly. "We'll prove your case. Vic has known you from the beginning of your career here in Texas. He can testify on your behalf."

"Oh, of course." Keri turned a brilliant smile on her attorney. "You know all about the partnership and the Silver Spoon company. Would you be allowed to be my lawyer and a witness?"

"Yes, that's possible. But it may never come to that," he said.

"What do you mean?"

GYPSY ENCHANTMENT

"We may be able to settle out of court," Vic explained.

Reid intervened. "Not at Keri's expense, we don't. Only if they drop the charges. She doesn't owe them a thing, and we'll definitely take them to court if they persist with this ridiculous charade."

Keri looked at Reid with a glow deep in her eyes. She had never had anyone defend her quite like that, and it was a heady feeling. For some reason, when a person has no family, few people have unqualified belief in that person's innocence. Only once before in her life had someone taken up for her solely on the basis of his own faith in her.

Tearing her eyes from Reid's, she spoke to Vic. "But I don't want to hurt Mack. He gave me my chance to get started, and it isn't his fault that things have gone sour. That wife of his, though, she's another story."

When Vic left, he kissed Keri's cheek and shook hands with Reid. "Since you're going to work on the case, where can I reach you if I need to?" he asked.

"Probably here during the day. I'm sure Marta will take a message for me if I'm out. At night, I'll be staying with Keri, of course. You can call me at her place," Reid said.

7

Reid ambled back to his chair to study the papers while Keri accompanied Vic to the door.

"Walk me to my car," he invited.

So she followed him down the steps and out into the parking lot. Still stinging from Reid's casual claim of possession, she was vainly trying to compose herself when Vic stopped by his late-model auto and turned to her.

"I take it he was someone very special in your life?" he asked with a peculiar gentleness in his voice.

Keri considered that. Then, "Yes, very special," she agreed.

The blue eyes darkened with worry. "I always sensed there was someone from the past, but you never seemed to want to talk about it. I respected your privacy."

She laid a hand on his arm. "You've been a good friend in every way, Vic."

"Let me finish, please, Keri." His handsome brow wrinkled in seriousness as he gazed down on her. "I sincerely want you to be happy—although I'm a little jealous that I'm not the one—but, when I met you, you were wary of men and involvement. I think you were hurt in the past, and I think Reid Beausan was the one who did it. Now he's back in your life, very much so, it seems. I don't want you to be hurt again."

Keri smiled up at the young attorney. "Thank you for caring, Vic. I'll be all right. Really. I know the risks." Her smile switched to a saucy grin that effectively ended the discussion. "Where would I be today if I weren't willing to take risks?"

Their words changed to the light quips of farewell and Vic drove off, leaving Keri to make her way slowly back to her office, her anger rising with each step up the stairs.

Smiling at Marta, she swiftly crossed to her room and closed the door behind her.

"How dare you act the possessive lover in front of Vic!" she began. "Why don't you wear a sign around your neck so all the world will see it at a glance: Keri's lover!"

Reid closed the gap between them, taking her shoulders in his strong grasp. "He's the one, isn't he?" he snarled at her.

She was shocked out of her anger. "The one what?" she asked stupidly.

"Your lover!"

"Vic is my very good friend. That's all!"

Reid looked disbelieving. "But he's the married guy you wanted to get involved with, isn't he?" He gave her a little shake.

"You're hurting me," she said, stretching the truth. His fingers were uncomfortable but not hurting.

Reid lifted her into his arms and carried her to the chair behind her desk, settling her on his hard lap. It seemed likely to become their place and posture of communicating while at the office.

"I'm sorry," he said, contrite. "I told you I was jealous of everyone close to you." Holding the gold knit of her sweater out of the way, he pressed warm kisses on her neck. "Did you miss me last night and the night before?"

"No. Yes." Winding her arms around his neck, she acknowledged the truth, to him and to herself.

"I missed you, too," he whispered, his bass voice husky. "Guess I'll just have to find a way to keep you by my side." A chuckle rolled over the words.

His hands stroked through her hair, caressed her body thoroughly, subjecting her to such sweet torture that she moaned slightly. His mouth found hers in a flaming kiss that lasted until they were both breathless. Lifting his head, he smiled with tender desire, causing her heart to turn over in her pounding chest.

"Now," he ordered briskly, "back to work. You carry on the daily stuff and I'll see what I can find out on this other thing. I want to go over your accounts, each and every one, with a fine-toothed comb. The ones for the partnership as well as for here."

"What are you going to do?"

"Get the facts to begin with. That way, we'll be able to prove our case. I'm going to go over your inventory, too."

Standing, he held her for another moment against his chest, his eyes searching the opaque darkness of hers as if for clues to some mystery only he knew existed. Then, he plunked her into the comfortable seat and told her what he would need.

Keri called Marta in and told her that Reid would be

helping solve the problem with Vivian. The secretary looked from one to the other and grinned. She volunteered to round up the records that he wanted to study.

Keri left them at it and returned to the task of catching up with a month's work, checking invoices and cash register receipts and deposit slips. Absorbed, she worked steadily through the afternoon while her lover did the same.

When he didn't show any signs of quitting as the hour hand on the clock passed five, then six, Keri went down to the kitchen and fixed them a light supper and carried it back upstairs. The building was quiet with only the two of them in it. She liked the sense of isolation with him.

Just the two of them, she thought with a yearning look at his head bent over the ledgers. If it could be that way forever. But it couldn't. One day at a time, that was all they had. A small panic washed over her, but she successfully quelled it.

Reid had accused her of running away. She wouldn't do that this time. She would outlast him. With this triumphant but heart-wrenching thought, she called him to eat.

After the meal, they decided that they had put in enough work for the day. Helping her lock up, he escorted her to the rental car that was the only vehicle left in the company parking lot. He whistled cheerfully as he drove until he hit heavy traffic.

"Damn!" he exclaimed as someone in a pickup truck with a gun rack mounted against the rear window cut in front of him. "You Texans drive like maniacs—seventy miles an hour and bumper to bumper."

Keri giggled at the complaint.

"The locals call this the spaghetti bowl because of the superhighways that run around town going every which

GYPSY ENCHANTMENT

way. Personally, I think Dallas-Fort Worth is scarier. So I headed for New Orleans instead." The gentle lines of her face became pensive. "And had that stupid wreck on the way."

Reid spoke quietly into her thoughts. "You'll have to direct me to your place from here," he requested.

Competently, she cued him on upcoming turns and lane changes he would need to make. Soon they were parked in her garage space at the five-story apartment building where she lived.

Reid opened the trunk of the car and took out a piece of brown luggage. The suitcase that she had left at his place wasn't in there. He saw her quick glance.

"We'll have to buy two sets of clothes if we do much traveling back and forth," he said, taking her arm and urging her toward the building. They went in and took the elevator to her floor.

Once in her apartment, Reid peered around expectantly, glanced into the kitchen and dining room, then went down the short hall and inspected the two bedrooms. He left his case in the guest bedroom.

"What are you doing?" Keri asked, surprise evident in her expression.

Reid's liquid gaze ran over her, making her feel that she was caught in a turbulent sea with a storm brewing. "I've looked for you twice now, following after your flight like a trained dog on a trail. If you want me in your bed this time, you'll have to issue the invitation."

Keri chose to ignore his statement; instead she pointed out the locations of towels in his bath and invited him to make himself comfortable. Then she quickly sought refuge in her bedroom behind the closed door.

Changing into a comfortable, modest caftan—she wasn't going to give him cause to complain that she tempted him beyond endurance—she contemplated his earlier statement. Reid was crafty. Very deftly, he had put the reins of their affair directly in her hands. Therefore, if things didn't go as she wished, she could only blame herself. She wouldn't be able to say he had seduced her. It was so much easier to be kissed senseless, she thought, but he had left the next move up to her. It was impossible for her to run away from him; there was no place left to run to.

After checking to make sure that he was in the living room, she grabbed sheets and made up the guest room bed, leaving the covers neatly folded back as the nurse had in the hospital. He would see from this that she wouldn't be rushed or coerced into a hasty decision. Frowning, she realized that her reasoning didn't even make sense to herself. She was always confused where Reid was concerned, except when he kissed her. Then she was very sure of what she wanted!

She joined him in the living room, sitting in one of the green velvet chairs rather than on the brocade sofa where he sprawled, already in pajamas and a knee-length robe. They watched a TV magazine program, then the early news.

Reid stood, yawned hugely and announced that he was going to bed. He had had to get up before dawn to catch his plane. He strolled off down the hall.

Keri turned off the television, checked the front door to make sure the dead bolt was fastened and went to her room. She was tired when she climbed into bed, but her eyes refused to close. She lay there listening to the whisper of air through the overhead vents. Finally, she drifted into a restless slumber.

An hour later, she woke, every nerve tense. She got up, tiptoed across the room and cautiously opened the door into the hall. A light shone from the living area. She decided to investigate.

Reid was in the kitchen, standing in front of the open refrigerator door. He looked tousled and grumpy.

"What is it? Are you hungry?" she asked.

He gave her a disgruntled, accusing look. "I can't sleep." His deep voice was gruff.

"I'll fix you some milk and cookies," she volunteered.

He shrugged and sat on a stool at the breakfast bar. She poured two glasses of milk and put out a plate of pecan cookies that she loved. Chef Paul kept her supplied with the treat.

After eating, she placed the dishes in the dishwasher and waited until Reid silently disappeared toward his bedroom, then she turned out the light and followed along to hers.

She was hardly settled before her door opened and Reid came in. He stood by her bed and glared down at her. "I can't sleep," he declared plaintively.

Swallowing hard against the sudden knot in her throat, Keri heard herself ask, "Would you like to join me?"

His sigh of relief was vast. "I thought you'd never ask."

She woke the next morning to the sounds of the shower and a bass voice singing about the yellow rose of Texas. Honestly, the man was incorrigible!

A slow smile curved around her mouth as she stretched and yawned luxuriously. His lovemaking hadn't been at all what she had expected. He had been slow and extremely gentle with her. It had given her an odd feeling, as if he were telling her of more than just desire. She just wasn't sure what the rest of his message was.

Feeling as new as the morning, she went to join her

lover in the bath. He welcomed her with a big smile and proceeded to soap her all over. It was a long while before they got around to breakfast and made a dash for the office.

That day set the pattern for the rest of the week. They worked late each night, ate most of their meals from Paul's trays that he sent up to them at lunch and at night, too.

Reid had left the office on Tuesday and returned with the records from the delicatessen that Vivian had been keeping in her possession under lock and key. He had breezily dismissed Keri's questions about his obtaining them.

"Honey, she couldn't keep them from me. You and Mack are partners, not her. I merely pointed out that a court order would be forthcoming to exclude her from the premises. A quick call to her lawyer convinced her I meant business!" He laughed at her frown of worry, kissed her nose and started on the ledgers and journals and inventory lists that he had confiscated.

Keri nibbled on her lower lip nervously and stared at his dark head bowed to his self-appointed task. He was doing this for her as well as keeping in touch with his own office. He was filling all the corners of her life with his dynamic presence. She would never be free of it.

What would he find in the records that he was going through? And what would he do about it?

On Friday, he threw down the pencil he was busy scribbling with and flicked her with a sultry glance. "Let's go out tonight, sweetheart. Dinner, maybe a show or dancing later?"

"Sounds good," she agreed.

They left right after the rest of the crew had called it a day and hurried off for a weekend of pleasure. At the apartment, they changed quickly, moving around each other in the bedroom and bath like an old married couple, completely at ease.

Keri's casual manner was a cover, though, for an inner worry and apprehension had been nagging since Reid had shown up on Monday and started going through the books. She was going to have to find out how much he knew from the delicatessen accounts . . . or how much he suspected. If necessary, she would head him off just as she had had to clamp down on Marta occasionally.

Reid took her to one of the most expensive restaurants in Houston. She wore a long black silk dress that was sleeveless with a short white jacket that had no collar or buttons. A black, gold and burgundy striped scarf was knotted casually around her neck in a loose circle, the ends falling free down to her waist.

Her evening shoes had very high heels, and her hair was piled on top of her head, adding inches to her stature. She looked like the sort of elegant companion a man of Reid's charm would prefer.

She waited until they had ordered and were served their seafood cocktails before addressing the subject that had been bothering her.

"So. Are you finding out anything interesting from all that deep digging you're doing?" she asked, dipping a plump shrimp in sauce and munching on it daintily.

"Um-hmm," he replied, bolting down an oyster after lifting it expertly from its half shell.

She waited, but he didn't elaborate. Taking a deep breath of annoyance, she held onto her temper and waited for a more opportune moment.

After their salad, but before the next course was brought, she tried again. "So what are you looking for, going back over all those old records?" The eyes that she turned on him were wide and entirely guileless. Her smile was warm and lovely.

He tasted the wine that the steward brought, approved it with a nod and flicked his cool glance back to his date. "Whatever comes up," was his uninformative answer. He draped an elbow over the chair back and surveyed the room as if he were a king making a quick check of his kingdom.

Keri restrained the urge to kick him under the table. As she reached for her wineglass he stretched his hands to hers, caressing the back of her knuckles with the tapering fingers that brought such pleasure to her senses.

A smile sneaked onto his mouth. "Don't worry about it," he advised quietly. His tone and gesture said he was in control of the situation. "I called Vic and arranged a meeting for Tuesday. I asked him to invite your partner and his attorney to join us."

She was startled. "What for?" she squeaked.

"I have a plan for settling this whole problem. One that should work out to everyone's satisfaction. Including yours. So quit worrying. I won't do anything you wouldn't approve of," he promised.

Their main course arrived. Reid refused to discuss business during it or later when they danced for a couple of hours before going home. That night he tucked her into bed beside him, kissed her goodnight and promptly went to sleep, leaving her stewing about his plans.

"What are your plans for today?" he asked her the next morning over a breakfast of waffles.

"I usually clean up the apartment, shop for groceries,

then goof off the rest of the weekend. Unless I have work at the office." She chewed thoughtfully on a bite of sausage.

"Let's go to the shopping center where your gourmet shop is. I've seen one deli, but I haven't had a chance to look over your pride and joy, yet."

She smiled broadly at him. "Okay, we can have lunch there. Saturday is one of our busiest days. The gourmet shop does almost as much business as the two delis combined."

They left the building a few minutes later, Reid driving the rental car. Keri hadn't gotten around to looking for a car for herself. She would have to do that soon.

"What kind of car are you going to get?" he asked as if he could read her mind. "Another Porsche?"

"Maybe," she said. Her mind wasn't on cars, but on his lean good looks.

He was dressed in jeans with a blue knit shirt that deepened the color of his eyes. His hair was still damp from their shower, and an aura of freshness surrounded him, enticing her with his clean-cut appearance and the subtle blend of fragrances that clung to him.

Swiveling her eyes to the passing street scenery, she again experienced that flutter of panic that bothered her whenever she realized how involved their lives were getting. This arrangement couldn't help but lead them both to unhappiness. Nervously, she smoothed the material of her slacks, wondering when Reid would tire of her.

Reid locked the car after they climbed out. He had parked near the front entrance. Now his attention was directed at the shopping center's construction; made of white concrete, it was massive and impressive looking.

Taking his arm, she led him to her attractive shop

where customers could buy a standard prepared box lunch or have one made to order. The prices were varied to suit a department store clerk's salary or the expense account of an executive.

There were two serving lines with mounted bars to push a tray along to the cashiers' registers. A separate register made it easy to buy from the wine and cheese racks without waiting behind those who were ordering lunch.

Keri loved the color scheme that was taken from her favorite bronze and yellow mums. A mural on one wall depicted a Hobie Cat, its striped sail puffed with wind, sailing on a westward course over a smoothly rolling blue sea.

The casual groupings of tables and chairs, which clients often rearranged to suit themselves, were interspersed with tall potted trees and bushy philodendrons.

Automatically, her eyes scouted the area, looking for signs of neglect. Everything was scrupulously clean. She lifted her chin with a pleased air.

"Proud, aren't you?" Reid teased her.

"Yes, I am." Her fingers dug into his arm. "Oh, Reid, I can't explain what this means to me. It's mine, something I did myself. I conceived the idea and brought it into being. Do you understand?" Her eyes glowed up at him.

"Of course I do. I remember how I felt when I closed my first big business deal after I took over my father's empire. Nothing since has compared with that first heady excitement." Catching her hand, he brought it to his lips for a quick kiss before urging her on. "Except you," he murmured.

She introduced him to the manager, a middle-aged man she had hand-picked for his sense of humor as much as for his no-nonsense approach to running the place. He was liked and respected by the staff, which he had hired. Keri hoped she could find people as capable as this man for the other shops when she bought Mack out.

"Eventually, I plan to go to a franchise operation. The managers who want to, can buy out their shops on a percentage basis each year. Naturally, I retain control of the name and have exclusive supply rights." She was outlining her future plans over lunch, which they were eating at one of her tables from the elegant black and silver boxes.

"You won't have to do so much work then, will you?" Reid quirked a brow at her. "You will have more time for other things?"

She shook her head. "Not me. I believe you have to keep moving or you stagnate."

"I'm not sure I believe that," he answered. "You have to slow down just to enjoy life. I'm enjoying being with you, Keri."

A frisson moved down her back. She was enjoying life now, too. Too much. Was this just a break for Reid, a short time of fun out of his usually busy life? A fling, delightful but not enduring?

Thoughtfully, she took a bite of her pita bread stuffed with cubed chicken and salad. She raised troubled eyes to find him watching her. Her smile was perfunctory.

She wanted to ask him how long he thought it would last. Her heart crumpled a little, losing some of its buoyancy. She wasn't really very good at living her life on a day-to-day basis. To get anywhere, a person had to plan and save and look far ahead. She saw no future for them.

"Reid . . ."

"Come on, honey. I want to take you shopping. That

red dress, remember?" He urged her to finish her lunch. He wolfed the last bite of his steak sandwich, drank the last swallow of iced tea in the paper cup and stood.

While she quickly ate the rest of her meal, he threw his debris in the trash can, came back to collect hers, then pulled her to her feet and swept her off down the wide mall corridors to a *haute couture* shop.

"Reid," she whispered, "I'm not dressed for this. And I can shop for and buy my own dress. You're not paying for it."

"This is my Christmas present to you, part of it. Now don't argue. You know you never win against me," he murmured as a beautifully dressed saleslady came toward them.

"We'd like to see some evening dresses," he announced in firm tones. "Red, if possible."

Knowing that he wouldn't be denied, Keri smiled sweetly at the woman whose dark eyes took in her casual clothes without a change in expression.

Chairs were placed at a spot close to a small stage with curtains behind it. Reid sat in one with his long legs stretched out and crossed in front of him. He viewed the dresses that were brought out, some worn by a model, some hand-carried for their inspection, and he vetoed one after another.

"Don't you have anything in red silk?" he asked an hour later in annoyance. "Something slinky?"

Keri managed to keep a straight face as the dark, expressionless eyes of the saleswoman roamed over her slight figure again.

"One moment, sir," the lady murmured. There was a whispered consultation behind the curtain. In a few minutes, the model came out in a charming red dress with a full skirt and a rounded, ruffled neckline.

"Good grief!" Reid exploded. "She's a woman, not a teenager going to her first ball." Grabbing Keri's hand, he rushed her from the shop so that she actually looked more like the teenager than the woman he claimed she was. In the corridor, she couldn't hold back any longer. She burst into peals of laughter while he looked rueful.

"Okay, what's your suggestion, smarty?" he demanded.

She led him to her favorite store, which carried clothes by her favorite designer. There she told the manager what she wanted, and in a few minutes, she and Reid were looking at three possibilities.

"I like that one." He indicated a flowing, flame-colored dress with a plunging neckline. "Try it on." With this imperious command, he sat down to wait for his order to be obeyed.

Keri went along to a dressing room where she tried on the dress. Standing on tiptoes, she had to agree that it was right for her. The neckline dipped in soft folds from gathered shoulders to a tantalizing plunge between her high, firm breasts. It flowed over her contours faithfully to the narrow waistline. In shifting iridescence, it swayed over her hips to fall in deeper folds around her ankles.

Still on her toes, she went out to show Reid, who nodded in satisfaction at her choice. She borrowed a pair of shoes and then stood patiently while the hem was measured for shortening to fit her petite height.

Reid paid for it with his credit card, not blinking an eye at the extravagant price. He was disappointed that they weren't taking the dress home. Next he insisted on buying accessories for it, then asked her to help him pick out Christmas gifts for his aunts.

Walking around an upper balcony, looking down on the ice skaters in the center of the mall and the domed roof above, Keri dreamily hummed a waltz tune as they headed for a jewelry store.

"Happy?" he asked, squeezing her hand in his.

"Yes, for now."

"Don't borrow trouble," he cautioned as if he read her doubts about their future happiness.

Putting her darker thoughts aside, she picked out silk blouses for the aunts plus some costume jewelry. Reid selected perfume for them and bought a new scent for Keri, too. When she protested his extravagance, he shrugged it off. "How many presents have I gotten to buy for you? We have ten years to make up for, woman, so don't argue!"

He bought a large shopping bag and dumped their purchases into it, then tugged her along to an ice cream parlor where she dithered between a banana split and a hot fudge sundae.

"Which are you going to have?" she asked.

He raised a suspicious brow. "Why?"

"Well, if you order the banana split, I can order the sundae, then you can give me some of yours," she reasoned.

Shaking his head, he told the waiter to bring one of each. After the young man left, he reached across the table to flick her nose. "I think you look like a teenager after all. No. More like a six-year-old waiting for Santa Claus," he decided.

Although she tried to hold it, the smile left her face. She pretended to study the skaters that were visible from where they sat.

"What is it?" he questioned softly, seeing her go solemn.

Glancing at him, then away, she lightly laughed. "What six-year-old believes in Santa Claus in this day and age?"

He thought this over. "Did you?"

"Not for long," she quipped.

Hands reached out, clasped both of hers that were playing with her napkin. "Why not?"

"Don't be silly," she frowned at him. "The older kids delight in cluing in the younger kids, whether in a family or a children's home."

"Is that what happened? Tell me," he urged gently. He wouldn't be appeased until he ferreted out the truth.

Finally, she told him. "It was nothing. I just didn't believe them, so I wrote Santa a secret letter and managed to mail it without anyone knowing."

"And then?"

"Well, what would you expect? I didn't get what I asked for. I wouldn't have, anyway. It was too expensive."

"What did you want?" he persisted.

She grinned at him, wrinkling her nose in sudden humor at her foolishness. "A red bicycle," she told him.

8

Over breakfast Sunday morning, Keri noticed that Reid looked rather grim as he read the paper. He had been strangely quiet since yesterday. She wondered what was wrong. The night before she had again tried to talk to him about his strategy in dealing with Mack and Vivian, but he hadn't wanted to discuss it.

She was very serious in her opposition to any exposure that might hurt her partner. Mack had been her friend, her only friend, when she was trying so hard to get started. Of course, his risk hadn't been all that great, since he did have an established business, but they could have overextended themselves in immediately expanding to a second deli while modernizing the first. They had used Keri's money in the venture. She knew that she could have lost her entire life's savings, and even though it had only been a few thousand dollars, the loss would have been devastating.

She knew almost from the first that Vivian was taking

items from the business. At the beginning, it had been little things: food and drink, a case of beer or a package of rolls. Later, it had been money or appliances charged to the deli that hadn't arrived there.

Keri had replaced the money from her own funds. The other things she had ignored. Mack didn't know all this. He had left the two women to handle the books and balance out the cash register.

Reid glanced up, saw Keri studying him with an intent frown on her face and smiled at her. Her expression became more serious. "What are you going to do on Tuesday, Reid?" She put her worries to him point-blank.

"Don't you trust me, sweetheart?" He laid the sports section aside.

"Of course I do!" Catching a strand of hair, she played with the curl with restless fingers as she tried to explain her position. "I know you want to help me, to protect me. So does Vic."

Reid's glance darkened and his face closed at this grouping of the two men into one category. "Yes?" he asked coolly.

"I just want you to realize that Mack was my friend, my only friend, for a long time. He was like a father to me in some ways. I don't want him hurt." She dropped the curl and opened her hands to Reid in a beseeching gesture.

"Do you think I'm going to crucify him?" he asked.

"No, but . . ." Her teeth chewed nervously on her lip. "But you tend to be autocratic. You run over other people's wishes if they don't mesh with your own." Her glance was one of resolve. "What I'm saying is: I will not let you ride rough-shod over Mack, not even to save me."

His voice was the rumble of thunder on the horizon.

"Is that the way you see me? As a brutal, insensitive manipulator? No wonder you were upset when I showed up again!" His crack of laughter was not humorous.

Taking a deep breath, she firmed her purpose to see this through. "No, I didn't mean that. It's just that you're very forceful, and you seem to get what you go after. But Mack . . ."

"Don't you think I understand your feelings for him? I'll respect those feelings, Keri. He won't know anything about his wife's double dipping."

Keri winced. "So you discovered it. I was afraid you would."

Reid nodded his head, his strong jaw tightening in anger. "It's rather obvious when the bank deposit is fifty dollars short one day compared to the cash register receipts, then a few days later, it's suddenly fifty dollars over and so the accounts are balanced for the month."

"What are you going to do when we meet with them? How are you going to keep Mack from knowing?"

Reid stroked away the line of anxiety on her brow. "I'm not sure yet. It's according to what information turns up on Monday."

"What kind of information?"

He grinned at her. "I'll tell you then. Can't you trust me?" he asked, a peculiarly wistful quality to his smile.

Her heart immediately softened toward him. "I do trust you as far as I'm concerned. I mean, I know you're on my side. . . ."

His grin took on a sardonic twinkle. "Well, at least you realize that much. Sometimes I've wondered about your perception." He opened his arms. "Come here," he invited.

Keri stared into the smoldering aquamarine eyes and wondered how they could look so cool and send flames of warmth through her at the same time. What did he mean by that crack about her perception? She perceived life very well, she thought. She saw it as it was, the reality versus the illusions.

His hand caught hers, and he pulled her to her feet and around the table into his arms. His lips nuzzled along her throat as if he were eating dessert, tasting and licking along the shallow depressions until she could no longer concentrate on anything other than him.

He untied the neckline of her robe and slipped his hand inside to massage her breast to aching fullness. Her nipple rose, hard and pulsing, a slave to his touch.

"Oh, Reid," she breathed, her fingers going instinctively to his dark, crisp hair to raise his head to her lips. Sure of her reception, she aggressively pressed her mouth to his, her tongue seeking his in ultimate bliss.

He rewarded her action by opening his lips to hers, letting her reach her goal without coy delay. His arms tightened about her, and his thighs became hard under her as desire surged through his masculine body.

Her hands slipped along his shoulders, caressing and kneading, as she explored the sinewy strength that was his. She welcomed the security of his greater mass as his body seemed to surround her own with his warmth and care.

His fingers moved again on her breast. Now they edged between her skin and the ruffled lace of her nightgown, sliding inside to caress the tender flesh with his direct touch. She gasped with the current of fire that spun away into the depths of her womanly passion.

"Let's go back to bed, baby," Reid crooned to her, lifting her in his embrace as he stood.

Her head pressed his cheek, and her arms clung to his broad shoulders as he carried her across the living room and down the short hall to their shared bedroom.

"I thought we would go to the beach at Galveston," she murmured, softly stealing kisses along the groove of his neck. "Maybe have a picnic and relax in the sun." She nipped his ear in a sharp lover's bite, then ran her tongue over the place.

"Later," he groaned. His eyes skimmed over her delicate figure as he stood her beside the bed and removed her robe and gown. He kicked off his pajama bottoms and, locking an arm about her waist, tumbled them both to the bed.

"I love to make love in the mornings when I'm fresh and rested," she told him as his arms enclosed her and pulled her into burning contact with his entire length. She skimmed her nails along his sides and onto his hips, drawing little circles of fire there that caused him to flame against her.

His leg parted hers, his thigh pressing her with intimate demand that brought an immediate response from her.

He kissed her cheek and to the corner of her mouth, his tongue flicking her skin with moist heat. "I've found you receptive at whatever hour we've come together," he teased huskily. "Warm and willing and welcoming. You accept me graciously and trustingly into your bed; why not in other areas of your life?"

Keri drew back her head to study his expression, but she could read nothing there. "What do you mean?"

He kissed along her neck. "Nothing," he muttered. "You're very generous with your body," he said in the tones of a compliment.

"But not in other ways?" she asked, a small note of puzzled anger creeping into the words. Her breath caught as his artistic fingers sketched a portrait of longing along her hips and legs.

He paused to gaze deeply into her angry eyes. "Do

you really think I ride rough-shod over people?" His voice was quiet, but she heard the emotion behind the question.

Astounded, she correctly recognized his pain. She had hurt him with her accusation! Her tender heart was at once stricken with remorse, and she stroked in soothing motions down his ribs and into the flat muscles of his abdomen.

"No, not really," she whispered. Then she said teasingly, "You always wear the velvet glove." She laughed softly as he grimaced.

"But over the fist of iron, huh?" He deliberately rubbed her neck with his raspy beard, bringing a giggle of protest to her lips.

Curving his body, he lowered his head until his mouth closed over her plump nipple. With tongue and lips, he sent her into spirals of erotic sensation that routed the last thought from her mind.

Forgetting work and its problems, the uncertainties of the future and her relationship with her demanding lover, she gave herself up to the intense, personal magic that he shared with her. He, too, was very generous with the pleasures of his body. She rushed headlong toward the exploding universe, wanting to capture it all now, before this moment, too, dissolved into eternity and was gone.

"Easy, baby," Reid pleaded as she moved wantonly against him, her hands goading him to accompany her flight. "Um," he groaned, "you know I can't hold out against you."

"Why try?" she asked with passion's logic. This was too wonderful to be put off. She urged him closer.

"I want it to last forever," he said, the words an enigma that she couldn't stop to figure out. "With you, I want it to go on and on."

GYPSY ENCHANTMENT

"It does," she whispered, lost in rapture. The morning sunlight settled in golden bands over her silken skin. He traced each spangled bar with a light caress.

His eyes, dark with passion, assumed a cryptic, almost moody expression in their depths as they roamed over her petite form. Her lashes opened over the smoky lucidity of her eyes to gaze at him with increased concern. She didn't understand him.

"What do you want from me?" she asked, suddenly very much afraid.

He stroked down her face with the backs of his knuckles. "Nothing, love. It's okay." His smile was a bright slash as he bent to her again. "This is what I want. This. And this."

His lips trailed fire along the surfaces of her skin that burned into an inner connection far within her heated body. Moving down, he distributed the magic flames over both her breasts, along her waist and into the curve of her side. Rolling her onto her back, he kissed her navel and chased a spark down an imaginary line along the middle of her tummy. Finally, he approached the gateway of desire and stoked the roaring furnace of their passion until she couldn't bear the ecstasy another minute.

"Please, Reid," she whispered, clutching his hair in desperate fingers and tugging. "Please, my love," she begged, incoherent in her need for him.

At once, his body was covering her own, pressing her against his entire length. For a long minute, his gaze washed over her, coming to rest on her eyes, which opened to return his perusal with a passionate gaze. He smiled tenderly. "Yes, darling. Yes," he answered her plea with a fervid promise.

His kisses became aggressive, showing his mastery over the situation and over her by taking them to the brink again and again. But he wouldn't satisfy her. Not yet. He held her in his hands, suspended in space, in a heavenly agony that brought forth sobbing cries from her throat.

"I want you, Reid." It was almost a protest.

"I know that, sweetheart. And you have me." He pressed heated kisses onto her red, swollen lips. "We belong. I told you that. You to me, me to you."

His words penetrated a part of her mind and created a small panic there. It was put down by the submerging quality of her longing.

"Oh, Reid," she whimpered.

"Tell me you belong to me. Only to me." His deep voice rolled over her like the fulminating crash of the sea.

Keri was caught up in his churning demand, was in danger of being swept away. Desire receded as she looked up into his face, confused by what she saw there. What did he want from her? Wasn't this enough? He had indicated that they would live each moment as it came. Was he asking for more? Was he demanding that she admit her love for him? Did he have to have that, too?

He closed his eyes over a flash of something that could have been pain. She wasn't sure.

"Never mind, darling," he said. "We have this. It's enough. For now, it's enough."

His strong body moved against hers, taking them to the stars once more, and this time, he let her catch one and ride its spiraling trail into the unbearable delight of passion's release.

She sighed in pleased exhaustion as he gently turned them to rest on their sides. She drifted into a light sleep and woke to feel his lips on her hair.

"What about that trip to the beach?" he asked.

GYPSY ENCHANTMENT

"Ummm." She protested movement. "We can go to the pool here at the apartment complex."

"No, I want to go to the beach now. Come on, sleepyhead. Let's go." He coaxed her out of bed and into her swimsuit.

They spent the afternoon exploring along the ocean side of Galveston Island, returning home in the early evening, tired, sandy and slightly sunburned.

On Monday, Reid spent the day on his own mysterious comings and goings, with frequent consultation with Marta that he didn't clue Keri in on. She was a little irritated with him over his secrecy, but she trusted his promise that Mack wouldn't be hurt.

He was out at noon, and she ate at her desk alone. She munched on the excellent chicken salad as if it were made of sawdust, paying no attention to its subtle flavoring.

Slender fingers touched her lips in an experimental way as she remembered their lovemaking of the previous day. There had almost been a quality of desperation in it. Was he getting tired of her? She had known from the beginning that passion wasn't enough to bind them forever. True, she felt more and more tied to him, but she didn't feel that he was bound to her in spite of his declarations that they belonged to each other.

There had been a searching probe from him for something more than they had shared. He had said that their passion was enough, then he had added the words "for now." What more did he want? Was he waking from his dream of the past as she had known he would and realizing that she wasn't what he really wanted?

A blackness, like a furious storm, covered her heart. He had never mentioned love to her. He had never said where he wanted their affair to go.

She squeezed her eyes closed. Where did an affair usually go? Nowhere. And that was the truth, the reality of life in that one word. Her lashes fluttered open, her gaze fastened to a point in the middle distance. Panic unfurled inside her and she had to press a hand against her aching chest to still it. She was becoming too dependent on Reid, on having him with her. Since moving to Texas, she had carefully maintained a distance between herself and all others, not letting anyone get too close. It was better that way. Safer. You didn't get hurt if you didn't get close.

Now Reid was back in her life. For over five weeks now, she had seen him every day, and for two weeks, she had been living with him in the most intimate environment, first at his house, then at hers.

It couldn't last. Soon he would have to go back to Louisiana. She would stay here. Then she would have to learn all over again how to live without him.

A small sob tore its way out of her throat, startling her with the sound in the quiet, empty room. Her apartment would be quiet and empty, too, when Reid was gone.

Quickly, she finished the meal and devoted herself to the task of straightening out a problem with one of her many suppliers. She wouldn't think of the future . . . or lack of one. Not until after Reid left.

He came into her office at five that afternoon. He looked tired, but his eyes were smiling.

"Did you get the information you wanted?" she asked, a faint apprehension running along her nerves at his triumphant grin.

"Don't I always get what I want?" he demanded of her. "Don't answer that," he added, leaning over her for his usual greeting. "Ready to go home?"

He ushered her out of the office and into his car. At

GYPSY ENCHANTMENT

the apartment, he helped her with their evening meal and rinsed the dishes afterward, stacking them with competent dexterity into the washer. They played backgammon and watched TV until bedtime.

"Come in," Reid said to Vic the next afternoon at one o'clock when the attorney presented himself at the office for a briefing and lunch before Mack, Vivian and their attorney, Mr. Black, arrived at two. It wasn't until they had completed the meal, however, that Reid told them of his researches and the results.

"First I noticed that money was coming up short in the bank balance at the deli, then it would be replaced a few days later. Then I noticed that Keri's personal account decreased by the same amount on the day the other one increased." His aquamarine eyes swung over to her.

"Maybe I was borrowing the money for a short period to tide me over," she suggested.

Reid shook his head. "That's not your style. If you don't have it, you do without. You're too honest, sweetheart, to play around with the accounts."

"There's no such thing as *too* honest," she said. "It doesn't come in degrees. You're either honest or you're not."

"You're also too loyal. You should have told Mack long ago instead of covering these losses yourself," Reid reprimanded her firmly.

Her chin lifted in challenge. "You said you wouldn't tell Mack . . ."

"I know what I said! I haven't broken my word yet, have I?" Reid's strong profile set in determination. "I'm just telling you what you should have done."

"Okay! I'm told!"

Vic's gaze swung from one to the other during this

brief exchange. A smile tugged at the corners of his mouth. He cleared the amusement from his expression. "So where does this get us?" he asked.

"I also found that several appliances were charged to the business account. They weren't at either store. I checked. Then, yesterday, dressed as a repairman, I checked the serial numbers of a dishwasher, a new clothes dryer and a food blender against the invoices at their house."

Keri was aghast. "How did you do that?"

"Marta called, found out that the esteemed Vivian was out, but the maid was in. I went over, said I needed to check the electrical connections on the items because some of them had gotten through with defective plugs and were a fire hazard. . . ."

"You idiot! You could have gotten into real trouble misrepresenting yourself like that!"

Reid scooted his chair close to hers. He took her hand and kissed the back of it in a gesture of gallantry that included his thanks for her concern.

The swift anger faded from her face, and her smile was tender and very revealing to the young lawyer who watched this exchange. "How do you plan on using this information?" he asked, bringing their attention back to the business at hand.

"We can't," Keri decided. "That's exactly what I don't want Mack to find out. He believes in her, and I won't have him hurt over a few dollars."

Reid intervened. "Will you let me handle this? I believe I can convince Vivian to drop her charges and keep Mack in the dark at the same time. Will you trust me?"

"Of course," Keri answered. "Have it your way. You always do." But this last was said on a teasing note rather than an angry one.

GYPSY ENCHANTMENT

A few minutes later, Marta announced the next visitors.

Vivian came in first. Her hair, a lovely shade of auburn, was set into an elaborate style on top of her head. Her dress was from a design house, and she carried a fur stole around her shoulders. Ultrathin brows arched smartly over her gray blue eyes. The couple's lawyer followed her. He was a middle-aged man, dressed in the legal uniform of dark, conservative suit and wing-tipped shoes. Mack came in last. His sparse gray hair was slicked back from his face, still showing the teeth marks of the comb where he had combed it into place while damp. With his rough face and paunchy body in slacks and casual shirt, he looked like a longshoreman on his day off. He didn't look at Keri as she made crisp introductions all around and invited them to be seated.

"You said you were interested in settling this without going to court?" Mr. Black opened the discussion.

Vic answered for his client. "Yes, we have certain information that we feel will convince you of the fairness of my client's offer."

Vivian made a snort of disbelief which quieted at a look from her attorney. Keri gave him points for being in charge.

"What type of information?" Mr. Black asked. His interest indicated that he was willing to listen.

"I believe that Mr. Beausan has the accounts and ledgers that will show you . . ." Vic's voice trailed off as he turned the show over to Reid. His blue eyes sparkled.

Keri gripped the arms of her chair as Reid lithely sprang up from his chair with a business ledger in his hand. He moved over to stand between Vivian and Mr. Black and proceeded to indicate the totals on the page.

Mr. Black got a puzzled look on his face, then leaned forward for a better look. His hard glance swiveled to Vivian, who bent over to gaze at the entry. She gasped audibly.

Mack heaved himself closer to have a look, and Reid casually turned the page. "Here," he pointed out, "are the totals of all income and expenses from the two delis during the first year of the Silver Spoon operation." He pulled out a loose paper. "Here are Keri's personal expenses and income as well as her expenses for the gourmet shop."

Smoothly, he continued showing them how much money she had made from the operations and how much savings she had used out of her account and how much she had started with.

When Mack lost interest in the figures, which he had never been very good at, Reid pulled out another sheet and showed it to Vivian and her attorney without a break in the flow of his explanation.

Finally, he closed the book and returned to his seat. "So, as you can see, all Keri's accounts are in perfect order. However, as a goodwill gesture and for the use of the established name of the deli, I'm going to suggest that she add to her offer a percentage of the profit from the two shops for the next fiscal year. Would you be agreeable to that?" he asked Keri.

Flicking her adversary a quick glance, she saw relief and greed replace the fear that Reid's skillful disclosure had brought to the haughty face.

"Yes, ten percent," Keri agreed. It was a small price to pay to get rid of the burden of Vivian's dislike and jealousy.

"She doesn't need to pay for the name," Mack suddenly said. "She's the one who made it. If it's worth anything today, it's because of her."

GYPSY ENCHANTMENT

Keri went over to him, bending in front of his bulky form. Her hands took both of his. "You gave me my start. You believed in me and my ideas. I couldn't have made it without you," she said softly. "I want to do it, if you're satisfied it's a fair offer."

He blinked his eyes, cleared his throat then nodded. "Yes, it's fair."

"Of course it is," Vivian said. "Of course we'll take it." She was now anxious to conclude the matter. Mr. Black's smile was rather puckish at this about-face, but he agreed that the offer was generous . . . in view of the cash flow indicated by the records. Vivian had the grace to color slightly.

A few minutes later, Keri was bidding the little party goodbye and giving Marta a wink as they trooped out. The secretary grinned hugely in reply.

After shutting the door, Keri spun around to face Reid, her eyes giving off sparks like flint on steel. She flung herself into his arms, which opened at once to receive her.

"Oh, Reid, you were wonderful! So cool! So in control! I was so proud!" she exclaimed while planting kisses on his strong jawline. Over her shoulder, her hero grinned at Vic, who watched this exuberant display with an indulgent grin.

"Honey, save some for later," Reid advised, easing her slightly away from his chest.

She stepped back. "Let me see what was in that ledger," she demanded.

Solemnly, he handed it to her, opening it at the first page that he had let Vivian and her attorney see but not Mack. It was the invoice for the clothes dryer, indicating it had been billed to the deli but delivered and installed at her home address. Other invoices appeared clipped to other pages as she flipped through the record.

Keri heaved a deep sigh. "I'm glad it's over. But I'm going to miss Mack, maybe even Vivian," she added wistfully.

The two men burst into laughter.

Vic gathered up his papers and stuck them in his briefcase. "If I ever have an enemy, I hope he's like you," he kidded her as he left. He kissed her cheek, shook hands with Reid, gave them both an approving smile and went out.

Reid dropped an arm around her shoulders. "Now, darling, it's time to think about heading back for Louisiana. I need to get back to the salt mine . . . and that's no cliché!"

"I understand," she murmured. "When will you be leaving?"

"Not me. Us," he said confidently. "You're going with me."

"No, Reid, I'm not," she answered quietly and waited for the explosion.

9

His brows lowered ominously over eyes that suddenly held a dangerous glitter in their depths. "All right," he said heavily, "I realize you have ends and pieces to tidy up here. When can you come? Friday?"

She swallowed nervously, trying to assure herself that there was nothing he could do to force her. "I'm . . ."

"I'll arrange to meet you, or if I can't come myself, I'll send Milton to the airport." He went right on making plans as if he didn't know by the obstinate set of her face that she had no intention of joining him in Louisiana.

"I won't be there Friday, either," she said quietly. Her eyes met his levelly, refusing to flinch in the face of the rising fury she recognized in his. She drew a shaky breath into her lungs, which were having trouble functioning.

"When?" he asked, his voice as soft as hers.

Her hand reached out for him, to console him and beseech his understanding. "Never," she whispered and clamped her teeth hard into her trembling bottom lip.

Reid turned swiftly and brought both his fists down on her desk with a crash that made everything on it leap into the air and settle in slight disarray.

"Dammit, Keri, why?" he demanded between gritted teeth, his voice still low but full of furious undertones.

Her arms locked around herself as if holding her body together, she walked away from the anger which he held in check with his superior willpower. Standing at the window, staring sightless into the street below, she told him, "I want it to end now. I don't want to drag it out to the point where we're both looking for excuses not to fly up for a weekend."

"I see," he said, his voice cynically cool now.

She turned, bravely confronting him, and saw that his mien was calm, almost smiling, as his eyes made a lingering survey of her face and figure. Her earlier fear returned; he looked more dangerous now than he had a moment ago when he had been consumed with anger.

"You must see . . ." she began reasonably.

"Oh, I see a lot more than you think I do," he assured her.

She ignored the interruption. "You must see that a clean break is better, easier on both of us." She gave a nervous laugh. "A long-distance love affair would soon be an unbearable strain," she advised him sagely.

"I quite agree." And saying that, he spun on his heel and walked out without another word.

Keri tottered over to her chair and sat down weakly.

GYPSY ENCHANTMENT

In a moment, she heard a car pull out into the street below.

He was gone, she thought. Just like that, without argument or force or anything . . . just gone. It was incomprehensible. It was . . . devastating. Her fingers twisted together in grief and the ache in her chest increased to a burning pain. Her somber eyes were very dark and opaque.

It was better this way, she told herself over and over as the afternoon wore on and there was no sign of Reid's returning. She became very quiet and soft-spoken as she talked to Marta about the estimates for replacing equipment. She made several important decisions that she had been putting off while the problem with Mack was still pending. Now there was no need to put anything off. She had to get on with her life. It was just that it didn't seem very much fun anymore.

She dictated several letters to Marta for their suppliers, signed some checks, wrote memos, filed her own records, and talked to Paul about the specials for the next week. Finally, it was time to go home.

She said good night to Marta and waited until everyone had left for the day before walking through the premises and locking the doors behind her. For some reason, instead of calling a cab, she slowly made her way out to the parking lot. The rental car was there.

Reid sat behind the wheel, his gaze fastened on her as she trekked the long-short distance between them. She opened the door and climbed in. Their glances met.

"Reid . . ."

"Hush," he whispered, taking her into his arms. "It's okay, baby. We'll do it your way. If this is the way you want it, this is the way it will be."

After placing her back into her seat, he started the

engine and drove off toward the apartment. "Is it all right for me to stay with you tonight, a sort of farewell party?" he asked politely.

"Yes, of course," she murmured, not quite sure this calmly smiling individual was the Reid she knew . . . the one who always got his way.

He was different, she thought, stealing glances at him as he guided the car through the home-bound traffic. There was an air of quiet resignation about him. He seemed to have accepted her decree. It made her sad.

Shaking her head, she tried not to think. The truth was, she didn't know what she wanted . . . not an affair but not this anticlimactic ending, either.

At her apartment, she started to prepare a meal, but Reid forestalled her. "Let's just go out for pizza," he suggested.

So they changed into jeans and went to a local pizza parlor and drank bitter red wine. Then they went home.

After the news went off, Keri turned off the television and stood there, waiting for Reid to make his next move. Smiling a little, he turned off the lamp on the end table and sauntered off to their bedroom. She followed a minute later.

Reid was already removing his clothing, dropping the items on the floor by the bed as he stripped. He brushed his teeth and finished his preparations for bed without speaking. She began to feel annoyed that he could be so casual on what was, after all, their last night together.

She went into the bathroom and took care of her nightly routine, slipped into a nightgown and demurely got into bed, turning out the light as she did. Reid lay on his side with closed eyes.

She felt his large hand caress her stomach, and with a

GYPSY ENCHANTMENT

soft sigh, she turned to him, snuggling into his embrace. Her hands pressed against his chest, feeling the even, hard pounding of his heartbeat as he pulled her closer. His breath touched her hair before his face lowered to find her lips.

His kiss was long, masculinely tender and passionately persuasive. In a while, he slipped her out of the gown so that their bodies could touch.

His lovemaking was everything she could want it to be. Neither of them withheld any part of their desire from the other. It was the very deepest, the most complete sharing between two human beings.

For long minutes, they lay in a half daze of exhausted bliss after they had climbed the final peak. Then Reid raised himself on an elbow beside her.

"Sweet gypsy," he murmured, "can you really walk out on this?"

With a belated dawning of understanding, she perceived just exactly what his intention had been. Using the passion that he could arouse in her, he had hoped to persuade her to continue their affair.

Her body became stiff. "You did that deliberately, didn't you, Reid? You thought you could use sex to force me to do what you want, but it won't work. I still mean it. This is the end!"

With a muttered imprecation, he swung away from her and out of bed. He pulled on his jeans in the dark, and then turned on the lamp and faced her after he gathered up the rest of his clothes. The look in his eyes was one of contempt.

"You have a pretty high opinion of me, Keri, to think I'd do that," he said in disgust. "But you're wrong. I don't want anything from you. Not anymore." He walked to the door.

"I'm leaving now." His voice became very soft. "I won't be back. You said I ride rough-shod over people. I'm sorry if you think I've misused you, but I just wanted to share something with you that seemed very wonderful to me. Maybe I'm the one who's wrong. Maybe it wasn't. Maybe it was just a dream from the past." He paused to study her somber expression, his eyes boring into her flint-dark ones that held no spark of hope.

He sighed, a rueful smile touching his lips, softening his strong jawline. "I forced you to stay with me once and I came after you when you left. I won't do that again. If you ever want me, you know where I'll be." He went to the phone and made his reservations. In a few minutes, he returned and packed his clothes.

"Do you want me to drive you?" she asked.

"No, baby, I can make it on my own. Unless you want the car."

She shook her head. He came over to the bed, kissed her once, lightly, and swiftly left the apartment.

His "Goodbye, gypsy" haunted the night long after he was gone.

Keri said good night to Marta and returned to her report. Finally, she laid it aside, pushing her chair around to stare out the window. The rain beat with slow monotony against the pane.

That was the way she felt, as if she were slowly crying inside. With thumb and forefinger, she pinched the bridge of her nose, trying to ease the tension of a persistent headache. It had been three days since Reid had walked out, and the weather had been dreary since then.

She cleared her desk, locked up and went out to the rented car she was driving while waiting for her new

Porsche to arrive. All the business ends of her life were neatly tied up now. It was only the personal ones that seemed to be dangling, she admitted when she walked into her empty apartment a half hour later. She switched on the TV just to hear the sound of another voice.

She made a sandwich and fixed a glass of Coke, then returned to the living room and watched the six o'clock news. After the local news, the scene flicked to one in Louisiana where flooding from unknown sources had trapped a team of experts in a salt mine. The men had been examining the site because of water intrusion, the reporter announced.

The wind and rain swirled about the man as he spoke from the mine site; spotlights and heavy equipment stood in the background. Keri sat stunned as she listened. It was Reid's mine.

Suddenly he appeared on the screen. Dressed in jeans and a Windbreaker, he paused to answer questions. "Yes," he said in his deep voice, "we know where the men are. There are three of them. We have an air pipe into the chamber, and we know they aren't injured. The water is chest high and rising. We're dropping a tunnel from above and at an angle." He demonstrated with movements of his hands.

"No," he answered another question. "It will be several hours yet. Probably tomorrow. I'll keep you informed."

For uncounted minutes, she sat there staring at the TV, her mind in a whirl. Her jumbled thoughts condensed into one compelling notion: Reid needed her. She knew it as surely as she lived and breathed.

Or did he? Once before, without thinking, she had gone to him when she had thought he would need her, but he hadn't. He had sent her away. If he hadn't had time for her back then, he certainly had no time for her now with this emergency on his hands.

She took her dishes to the kitchen, rinsed them and put them in the washer, suddenly remembering the times last week when Reid had insisted on cleaning up the kitchen after she had done the cooking. A fair division of labor, he had called it.

She returned to the living room and paced the floor, her thoughts in confusion. She wanted to go to Reid. Deep within her was a need to comfort him that she didn't understand. Was it part of a nurturing instinct that she'd never suspected in herself? Or was it simply a part of loving, a way of caring for her man?

He would probably regard her arrival as a capitulation on her part to his demands that they continue the affair. Or maybe he wouldn't want her at all now.

What harm could it do to go there and find out? her practical self inquired. If he sent her away, well, then she'd know. She would go on and get it over with.

She checked her purse for money. Almost a hundred dollars in cash plus a large balance in her personal account. And she had her credit cards. Calling the airport, she found there was no immediate flight out.

Undaunted by this, she dialed a charter plane service. Then she packed a large suitcase with several changes of clothing. She didn't know how long she would be gone. Hesitating, she looked at the red silk dress that was now hanging in her closet. She decided to take it, too. Last, she called Marta and told her what had happened.

"Go to him," Marta said.

Keri did. First she took a plane, then she grabbed a taxi to the mine site. The guard wouldn't let her in the gate.

"Would you please tell Mr. Beausan that Keri Thomas is here?" she asked with desperate patience.

"He's busy, miss. I can't disturb him," the conscientious man stated firmly.

Holding on to the wire of the high fence, she peered through the rain and dark toward the buildings. She saw a familiar figure. "Reid," she shouted. "Reid!"

He froze, then his tall form was running over the wet ground. Sweeping past the guard, he crushed her in his arms. "Keri," he said. "Keri."

Taking her with him, he started back inside. "My suitcase," she said. He grabbed that, too. In his office, he dialed a number, then pulled her against him while waiting for it to answer. He kissed along her cheek.

"Tears?" he questioned, licking his lips.

"No," she denied.

"Salty rain, Keri?" His attention was diverted to his call, and he talked for several minutes about getting two more pumps to the site. Then he hung up and immediately dialed another number. "I'm calling Milton to come take you home," he explained.

"I want to stay with you," she protested.

"I'd rather you wait at the house. That's enough, just to know you're there, waiting for me," he said huskily.

Raising damp eyes to his, she nodded. He kissed her once and raced off into the night while she sat on a hard chair and marked time in infinitesimal segments until Milton came for her.

At the house, the butler carried her bag into the master suite without hesitation. Keri followed, admiring the holly and red velvet bows entwined along the banisters. She had forgotten to decorate her apartment for Christmas, she realized.

"Would you like coffee in the library?" Milton asked.

"Yes, please, but I'm going to shower first."

Alone, she removed her damp suit, took a hot shower and put on a gown and warm, quilted robe of deep rose. Going downstairs, she paused to look at the Christmas tree in the living room before slipping into the library to wait.

At midnight, she drifted up to bed and, after a long time, into a restless sleep. It was dawn when Reid came home.

He took a quick shower and slid into bed beside her warm body, pulling her securely against him.

"Did you get the men out?" she asked.

"Yes, thank God," he whispered fervently. He kissed her cheek near her mouth. Then he was asleep.

Smiling, she nestled her cheek on his chest, laying an arm across him in a protective manner. In another minute, she was sound asleep, too.

He was still sleeping on Saturday afternoon. Keri ate a quiet lunch by herself, then strolled down the hall to the library to wait. She heard the doorbell ring and Milton's voice as he answered. "In the library," she heard him say.

A second later, Aunt Hester strode in. "Isn't this perfectly terrible weather," she complained with a smile that belied the words. She kissed Keri's cheek and pushed her back into her chair. "Sit down, dear. How are you?"

"I'm fine," Keri said, happy to see Reid's delightful relative.

Hester looked lovely in a red pants outfit, making Keri aware of her drab appearance in tan jeans and a long-sleeved sweater of mint green. The woman sat in a comfortable chair and, in a businesslike way, began to catch Keri up on all the news of the last couple of weeks.

GYPSY ENCHANTMENT

Milton brought in a tray with coffee and a plate of eclairs. Hester insisted that Keri play hostess.

"I think Reid would expect it of you," she said warmly, bringing a blush to Keri's smooth cheeks. "I'm glad you're back. I understand from Mrs. Jannis that Reid was a bear to live with the past few days. She was almost glad he had an emergency to occupy him and take him out of the house." Hester laughed gaily, reaching out to pat Keri's hand. "You mustn't do him that way."

Keri gazed into her cup, embarrassed because Hester obviously thought they had had a lovers' quarrel. Did his aunt think that they were engaged? How could she tell her that they were simply having an affair?

Well, that was Reid's problem. She refused to be responsible for explaining her presence to his relatives —although there didn't seem to be any real difficulty. Both his aunts accepted her without question into their nephew's life. Maybe this was the usual thing with his mistresses?

No, she wasn't going to think of the past. One day at a time was the way she would take their relationship. Reid had told her that himself. And from now on, she was going to play it his way. What he wanted, she wanted, too. She thought she had conceded that point when she came to him.

Looking up, she discovered Hester's kindly gaze on her, and she murmured, "We had a misunderstanding."

The gray feather-cut hair bobbed up and down as Hester nodded. "I thought so. I'm so glad that you didn't let it stand in your way. Reid needed you," she said firmly.

"Yes, when I saw the news on TV, I had to come." She smiled tremulously at the other woman.

GYPSY ENCHANTMENT

Hester's gentle face took on a pensive mood as she became lost in her thoughts. "I wish . . ." She broke off to sigh deeply.

"You would like to be friends with your sister, wouldn't you?" Keri asked with sudden insight. "That's why you came back here after your husband died. You wanted to be with your family."

"There's so few of us, you see. Only the three."

The bright red vest lifted in another heartfelt sigh. Keri experienced a wave of sympathy and wished she could help. She snapped her fingers. Hester started, then looked at her questioningly.

"Reid's party is the twenty-first. . . . Why, that's tomorrow, isn't it?" she exclaimed in delight.

"Yes, that's right," Hester said.

"Do both you and Amy attend? She doesn't stay away because of you, does she?" Another thought occurred. "You don't take turns, do you?"

Hester said, "We both come, but we don't talk to each other."

"Well, that's it," Keri decided. "If I can get you two together and guarantee you privacy, would you be willing to try to talk to her?"

"Yes, but it won't work. She walked out the one time I attempted that stratagem."

"When was that?"

"Back when I first moved here. . . ."

"That was too close," Keri broke in. "She wouldn't console you for your loss. She didn't think you deserved it. She had lost him long before."

Hester's brows rose in surprise at the notion. "I never thought of it that way."

"Listen, Aunt Hester, come an hour early tomorrow, okay? I'll invite Amy to come help, uh, arrange flowers Does she do that?"

GYPSY ENCHANTMENT

Hester shook her head negatively. "Not Amy." Her brow furrowed as she tried to think of something that Amy might need to do in order to get her here early. "The problem is that Mrs. Jannis and Milton have been handling these parties for years. They go like clockwork."

"Surely there must be something," Keri cried. She racked her brain. "If only Reid would wake up . . ."

"Do I hear my name being taken in vain?" a bass voice inquired lightly. He stood in the door dressed in casual attire and loafers.

Keri's face lit up. "Oh, Reid, we're just trying to think up an excuse to get Aunt Amy here early tomorrow."

The dark brows rose inquiringly. "Pour me some coffee, will you? Why do we need her here early?" He slumped onto the sofa beside Keri, his hard thigh pressing slightly against hers. "Good morning, Aunt Hester. Or is it afternoon?" He peered out the window with an exaggerated squint.

"Afternoon. Here's your coffee." Keri handed him her cup with an impish grin. "Hester wants to talk to Amy in private."

Aquamarine eyes that looked like they were used to seeing far distances glanced from one woman to the other. "I see," he said slowly. "This smacks of conspiracy and collusion. And right here in my own house while I so innocently lay in my bed sleeping . . . oooof!"

An elbow in his side cut off his melodramatic speech. "Are you going to help us or not?" Keri demanded.

Making a face, he rubbed his ribs. "I don't think I have a choice. We'll invite her over for an early supper with us before the festivities begin. How's that?" He glanced proudly around the room.

"Oh, good!" Keri was pleased.

Hester laughed at the two young lovers. Her eyes

165

misted over. "You remind me of Ralston and me when we were your age. Oh, it's so good to have youth and laughter in this house again!" she exclaimed. Her delighted smile brought an answering solemn one from Keri and an enigmatic one from her nephew. She stood up and the couple did likewise.

"I must go. What time do you think I should come tomorrow?" she asked Reid.

He considered. "We'll eat at seven. Come at seven-thirty. That will give you an hour before the party. Either you'll have to repair your makeup after you talk to her or else we'll have to bind up your wounds," he quipped.

They walked his aunt to the door and waved her off; then arm in arm, they returned to the library. He pulled her into his arms inside the door. She pressed away from him. "Call your Aunt Amy first," she reminded him.

Amusement glittered over her in his glance. "Afraid things will get out of hand and I'll forget, huh?" He took her hand, pulled her over to the desk and picked up the telephone.

Impatiently he dialed the number, then pulled Keri back into his arms. He kissed her hotly all over her face, avoiding her lips when she would have kissed him, too.

"Hello, Aunt Amy? This is your favorite nephew here. What do you mean, who? How many favorite nephews do you have?" He winked broadly at Keri as he joked with his aunt.

Grinning, she sighed to herself over how handsome he was, how much she loved him, what his caressing fingers were doing near her breast. He was in such high spirits now that his emergency was over and the men were safe. Her own spirits rose to terrifying heights just being near him.

GYPSY ENCHANTMENT

"Keri and I wanted to invite you to have an early supper with us tomorrow night. Can you come at seven? Yes, she's back." His eyes cut to Keri, studied her face with lazy passion. He chuckled at something his aunt said. Then, "I'll let you know as soon as I know the answer to that one. I certainly hope so!" He laughed again, said goodbye and hung up.

"What did she say?" Keri demanded.

"She'd love to have supper with us. Do I get a kiss for a reward?" He pursed his lips and held his face down to hers, letting her reach his mouth.

When she gave him a demure smooch, he caught her up against his chest and moved over to the sofa with her. He placed her in the corner. "Stay there," he ordered and plopped down beside her. Then he ate two eclairs and drank two cups of rather cold coffee. Then he turned on her.

"You're next," he muttered with obvious meaning. He leaned his weight on her, mashing her into the confining space.

"Reid, you're crushing me!" she gasped, giggling and trying to elude the marauding mouth that was biting menacingly at her.

He lifted her and placed her willing body in a prone position and tugged off her shoes. He kicked off his own and lay down beside her, partially covering her petite form with his own.

"Hmmm," he nibbled on her cheek for a long minute. Holding his head up, he squeezed one breast, then the other as if checking fruit for ripeness. He felt of her waist and patted her thighs and made a couple of other intimate forays.

"What are you doing?" she asked.

"Just making sure everything is where I remembered it," he said in self-satisfied tones.

"It's only been a few days," she remonstrated.

"But it seems like years." His lips covered hers, making retort impossible.

With all the subtle mastery that he was capable of, he reestablished their need of each other, making her know fully that she belonged to this one man.

"Oh, Reid," she breathed in a sigh of ecstasy when he finally released her mouth from a thorough exploration. "Umm, you taste of chocolate," she whispered, twining her fingers in the smooth helmet of his hair, ruffling it into disorder.

"Ahem," a voice said from the doorway. "Do you need any more coffee, sir? Or would you like breakfast?"

Reid raised his head from the spot on Keri's neck that he was tantalizing. "No, thank you, Milton. We've had plenty. You may take the tray. And close the door when you go out, please."

"Very good, sir."

Milton crossed the floor on silent feet, picked up the cups and plates, replaced them on the tray and carried the whole out, closing the door behind him.

"Ohhh," Keri wailed. "What must he think!"

"That I'm about to make love to you and don't wish to be disturbed," Reid supplied calmly. He found his spot again.

"Reid . . ."

Again his mouth took the words from her lips. He brought fire to her senses once more. And he was right. It seemed years since she had last been in his passionate embrace.

His artistic fingers kneaded a warm spot onto her hip before sliding around her and under the waistline of her pants. He massaged the firm flesh of her buttocks, thrilling her with the skill of his movements. "I can never get enough of you," he murmured into the thick tangle of her hair.

"Me, either," she whispered incoherently, but he understood the meaning.

"We belong together, don't we?" His breath brushed flames along her temples as he kissed from one to the other across her tightly closed eyes.

"Yes, oh, yes," she agreed.

Her fingers pushed under the fleecy sweatshirt he wore, finding the warm skin of his back. With the very tips, she explored along each ridge and groove, learning his form through her touch until she knew the textures of his body better than she did her own.

With a low groan, he pulled from her arms, holding her hands away to prevent her from clasping him tightly again. "Let's talk, baby," he requested.

She opened disbelieving eyes. "Talk?" Scrunching up against the end of the sofa, she pulled her sweater down over her bare breasts. "About what?"

"Us. Are we going to try to make a go of this torrid affair of ours?" His keen gaze never left her eyes.

"Yes, I think so. Yes," she nodded emphatically. That was what she had decided, and once she made a decision, it was full steam ahead for her. She pursued her goals with single-minded devotion. "If that's what you want," she added.

"Very much." He quickly laid that question to rest. "It will mean planning our schedules so that we can be together all the time. Not more than an occasional night apart."

"Can we do that?" she worried.

"I think so. I have some ideas about consolidating our interests, but we can discuss the details later. Right now, I just wanted to be sure you were with me."

"Yes," she averred. She gave him an especially

brilliant smile, feeling good and secure for no reason at all.

Reid smiled at her, but it was more like a caress. Then his eyes resumed their smoldering perusal of her, and he moved close, sliding his hands under the mint green top to cup her breasts until they came to passionate fullness under his touch.

Keri grasped his broad shoulders, pulling him to her, placing frantic little kisses along his jaw that was still smooth from his recent shave.

With a spinning move, Reid turned them so that she was sitting in his lap, her head pillowed on his arm.

"Who says there's no Santa Claus?" he whispered. "I'm getting all my Christmas wishes."

10

Keri's cheeks needed no additional color, she decided the next night as she put on her makeup. Carefully, because her fingers were trembling a little, she outlined her eyes with brown-black pencil, bringing out their volcanic darkness and enhancing their size and shape. Reid came out of the bath wearing a towel around his middle. She frankly ogled his handsome masculine physique until he caught her, then she quickly went back to her task.

He came over to her, bending to push her hair out of the way and deliver several spine-tingling kisses to the back of her neck. "What are you wearing? It turns me on!" He bit her neck, eliciting a squeal of laughter and protest.

"It's the perfume you bought me in Houston, remember?" She craned her neck up to look at him with a backward glance. "Also the dress and shoes."

"That dress is beautiful on you." He sounded awestruck. His hands followed the soft folds that widened over her breasts, then narrowed again to her waist.

Keri laughed happily. "Very well put, sir!" she exclaimed. "Most men say a woman looks beautiful in a dress, giving the outfit credit for the increased loveliness."

Reid shook his dark head. "It isn't the dress. I know that you're beautiful without anything at all on, but silk is just material until it's draped over this luscious figure." He gently explored her curves, being careful of the silk.

She arched a brow. "Are you going to wear anything to your party? I mean, I know it's a sort of birthday party, but are you planning on wearing your birthday suit?" Her coyness disappeared into peals of laughter at the sardonic expression on his face as he moved over to his chest of drawers.

Keri quickly finished with her eyes and lips and stood to survey the total effect. The red silk swished all around her with every movement. The diamanté bows on her satin slippers twinkled from beneath the skirt with each step. She was the picture of an enchanted princess, she thought.

She turned to the man who watched her with that leashed passion visible in his eyes and made him a curtsy. Her smile faded into a thoughtful countenance.

"Reid, would you leave me alone with your aunt after we eat?" She assumed a worried look. "I don't think we should spring Hester on her without some warning. Some type of preparation might make her more receptive, although I feel, in my bones, that she's lonely, too."

"Too?" he questioned the adverb. "As Hester is lonely . . . or as Keri is lonely?"

Momentarily she was thrown into a confused panic

by his question, then she recovered. "How can I be lonely? Haven't I got a lover who demands every minute of my time?" She gave him a flirting glance from beneath her lashes.

"That's right!" Slipping into his shirt, he began whistling softly as he finished dressing.

Keri affixed his cufflinks, held his jacket for him and together they went down to wait for their guest. In the library, Reid settled himself comfortably in his favorite chair while Keri hovered here and there, unable to relax.

"Don't be nervous, darling. Everything will be fine," Reid soothed her in his wonderfully deep voice that could probably calm the sea in the throes of a hurricane. Keri ruefully acknowledged that she was worried about the sisters. Reid knew her better than any person ever had.

When Amy arrived, they both went to greet her. The woman was wearing a dark-blue long skirt with a severely tailored jacket that was saved from seeming puritanically plain by the richness of the velvet material and the froths of lace that cascaded down the front.

"How lovely to see you again!" she greeted Keri, hugging the younger woman before embracing her nephew, who began shepherding the two females toward the dining room.

Because of the demands of the party, the evening meal was a simple one served in the breakfast room; the dining room table was laden with the party treats. Reid answered Amy's questions about the salt mine, explaining in detail what had happened.

Keri hardly tasted the excellent beef and vegetable casserole that Mrs. Jannis had prepared for them. Her mind fretted over what she should say to Reid's aunt. She didn't want to make her angry or hurt her, either.

GYPSY ENCHANTMENT

Well, she heaved a mental sigh, the truth was probably the best—when all else fails, tell the truth!

At a signal from Milton, Reid stood. "I have a call I need to make. Why don't you two join me in the library when you finish your wine?" He strolled out, giving Keri a thumbs-up sign as he went out the door.

Milton removed their plates and quietly disappeared. Keri fingered the stem of her wineglass. She took a deep breath to start the conversation.

"I'm quite looking forward to the party," Amy said. "It's always a highlight of the year for me."

"Hester is here," Keri said. She saw a tensing of the slender body in its blue velvet. The lace at the neck quivered slightly. For a moment, she was afraid the older woman was going to stalk out.

"Yes, she always comes," the aunt replied.

Keri licked her lips. "She's here now. In the library. To see you. Aunt Amy," she continued quickly, before she lost her nerve, before the woman told her to mind her own business, "please see her. Talk to her. Don't . . . don't throw away the chance to be friends," she pleaded.

Amy shook her head. "Hester doesn't want to be friends with me," she said, her voice sad rather than angry. "I . . . she tried once, a long time ago, and I . . . cut her off, rather cruelly."

The worry dissolved out of Keri. The feeling in her bones had been the right one. "She would understand, I'm sure. Would you try this time? Don't forget, you are sisters. You have a childhood in common. I know you were close back then. She said you were. Family ties are too lasting, too important to just let wither away. Would you go talk to her?"

Keri held her breath, watching as emotion poured in

changing tides across the patrician features. Finally, the gray eyes lifted to Keri.

"I wouldn't know what to say," she protested faintly.

Keri took heart. It wasn't an out-and-out refusal. "Just say, 'Hello, sister,'" she suggested. "Come on. Now's a good time. You have an hour."

Leading the way, she coaxed Amy to the library door, opened it and stood aside. She caught a glimpse of Hester's still figure across the room. Amy stepped over the threshold. There was a moment of silence. Then, "Hello, sister," they said in unison.

Keri closed the door.

Reid stood down the hall, a strange solitude about him as he watched the brief tableau played out. When Keri turned, he opened his arms and she rushed to him. She was trembling.

"Hold me, Reid," she whispered, needing him in a way she couldn't remember needing anyone before.

"It's all right, love," he assured her. He kissed her hair, along her temple and then her lips as she raised her face to his.

Her arms crept around his neck, and she wished the night was advanced, the party over and she was held secure in his arms in their bed with all the world shut out. It frightened her, this intensity of yearning.

With a supportive arm around her, Reid guided them into the living room where they waited until his guests started arriving. He kept Keri at his side, introducing her to everyone. Some of the people she vaguely remembered from her work in the restaurant.

"Keri used to be a Louisiana girl, but she moved to Houston and made her fortune," Reid was saying to a Mr. Parren and his wife. The man was manager of the Beausanville thread mill.

"Well, maybe we can figure out a way to tempt her back," Mr. Parren said in jovial tones.

Mrs. Parren looked Keri over with speculative interest. "I'm sure Reid can handle it," she murmured with a little laugh catching her tinkling voice.

Reid grinned widely. "I'm working on it, I'm working on it," he teased, bringing an added surge of color to Keri's face.

It was over an hour later that the two aunts drifted into the crowded living room. They weren't arm in arm, but Keri noticed a suspicious brightness to their gray eyes and a tinge of pink along their nostrils. Reid nudged her side, smiling significantly down on her.

"What do you think?" she whispered.

He bent to her ear. "Looks good, doesn't it?"

The women came to them. Hester clasped Reid while Amy put both arms around Keri's petite form and hugged the girl to her breast.

"We've been such fools," Hester grandly admitted. "Each of us wanting to speak to the other but letting fear hold us back."

"Not without cause," the practical Amy reminded the loquacious Hester.

"True. Well, we get it honestly. All Beausans are stiff-necked. Always have been."

"Father wasn't too bad," Amy said.

Hester agreed. "But he had Mother."

Keri maintained a smile while the three relatives discussed the merits of various ancestors. Remembering their manners, they soon split up to mingle with the other guests.

It was nearly midnight when Keri went upstairs to freshen up. When she returned, she watched the members of the party, wearing their holiday clothes and faces, ever-moving in a changing pattern like an intricately choreographed dance.

A lovely girl, young, with sun-streaked hair and a dazzling smile, clung to Reid's arm. He was smiling down at her with a fond, indulgent ambience about him.

A stab of pain hit Keri so unexpectedly that she nearly staggered under the blow. Swiftly she walked down the hall, into an empty room and out the side door onto the patio. Like a wraith of the night, she glided across the smooth, hard stones to stand at the balcony where she could see into the living room. Reid was still talking and laughing with the girl.

The two aunts were together amidst a group of people who were obviously brimming with Christmas cheer. Milton, with a faint smile on his imperturbable face, moved on his quick cat-feet among the crowd.

A moth flew at the light spilling from the glass door again and again, beating itself to death against the invisible barrier. Keri watched it with macabre fascination. Her gaze pierced the barrier to the people inside. She was like the moth, she thought. Forever on the outside. What was the key that could open the invisible wall?

She knew the answer. Reid's love. The thing she had never dared to hope for. It was something she would never have. And because he would never love her, he would never marry her. Marry. She repeated the word as if it were a rune that mortals weren't allowed to invoke.

She turned away from the house and followed the steps and the path until she came to the canal. She walked along its grassy bank in the moonlight, feeling infinitely alone and lonely.

Reid would marry someone like that girl, someone of his background, not a self-made fast-food entrepreneur. Who could blame him? Who wanted someone with all her doubts and complexes, an orphan who didn't even remember her parents and had no other blood ties that she could find?

She wanted to leave, to go back to Houston where she had found a measure of safety. But she couldn't. She had told Reid that she would stay with him for as long as he wanted her.

Pressing the back of her hand to her forehead, she thought of her options. She would stay until after the holidays. Then she would go back to Houston. Gradually she would lengthen the time that she stayed away, especially as she perceived signs that Reid was getting tired of the affair. Somehow she would know when the final break came. She would simply return to Houston and stay. Or Reid would come back here, and they would both know it was the end.

She clenched her hands against her chest. The burning pain had returned as if her lung were torn again. This time it was her heart that was punctured.

"Running away?" A voice spoke from the shadows.

Keri whirled to face the tall form. "Reid! You startled me!"

"You didn't answer my question." There was a brittle note in the dulcet tones.

"I, I just came out for some air," she said.

"But you were thinking of leaving."

How had he known that? "Don't be silly," she denied. "What are you doing out here?" She tried to change her defense to offense.

"Looking for you. Our guests are leaving." He took her hand and walked with her to the house, his clasp firmer than it had to be.

GYPSY ENCHANTMENT

The leave-taking, spurred by a signal from Reid to his aunts, proceeded in a leisurely fashion until the last couple had departed. Keri and Reid stepped back into the house from the doorstep where they had been waving the final farewell.

"Let's go into the library," Reid said. The controlled quality about him was one of anger, not passion. A tremor ran along every nerve in Keri's slender body.

While Keri sat in the snug corner of the sofa in the large book-filled room, Reid paced the floor in front of her for several seconds before rounding on her. "Why are you thinking of leaving?" he demanded.

She fingered the folds of her skirt. "I don't know what you're talking about."

"Come on, Keri," he barked impatiently. "What has panicked you? What emotion has gotten too strong for you to handle? Why do you want to run out?" The lancing beam of his bright gaze pierced her armor, leaving her wounded when the battle had hardly begun.

"I'm not going to run out. I said I would stay." Her blood rioted through her veins as she recalled her promise. Her voice came out trembly instead of firm as she meant.

"Good!" he grated. He stalked across the room. "What am I going to do with you?" he asked, spinning back to glare at her.

Anger began to balance the fear that she felt. What was *he* so upset about? She lifted her dark, opaque eyes to him, bravely facing his incomprehensible temper. "What do you want me to say?" she cried. "What do you want from me?"

What more could she give him? He had her love; she had promised her life and body to him as long as he wanted them. What else was there?

GYPSY ENCHANTMENT

Slowly he approached until he stood no more than a foot from her. Something like pain defined the lines of his strong face. He spoke softly. "I want you to love me as I love you," he said. "I want you to admit that what we have is something special that transcends time and circumstances." He cast a piercingly sharp look at her. "Isn't it?" He dared her to deny his statement.

She could only stare at him in wonder.

"I want you to know that we belong, and I want you to be *happy* about that, not resentful or angry or whatever you seem to be. Do you understand?" he barked at her.

Keri pressed both hands to her aching throat. "No," she said in raspy tones.

His head swung in a negative shake, indicating his irritability with her unfathomable reasoning. He continued, "And I'll tell you what I don't want!" He fixed her with a hard glare. "I don't want you running out on me every time you get upset . . . or whenever your own feelings get too strong to be controlled and you get scared."

"I don't know what you're talking about," she again protested feebly.

"Don't you?" His grin was almost satanic, and panic scurried around in her like startled forest creatures looking for a hideaway.

She tried to muster her courage to ask him about his statements about love, but there didn't seem to be any of that emotion present in his demeanor. He seemed intent on punishing her.

His smile became tender. "Think about it," he commanded softly.

Think? When her mind and heart were stunned into immobility by this alternately raging, smiling, completely devastating lover!

"And another thing," he added, "I don't want you to accuse me of living in the past or of reaching for a dream when I'm feeling nostalgic or when I try to be romantic by taking you to places where we've been together at other times. That's a lover's prerogative!"

Deep in the flint-dark eyes, a fire was beginning to glow, the flames sending out a curling warmth of hope throughout her trembling body.

"It's little things like that that bind people together—the shared memories, the little private jokes. It isn't me who's living in the past; it's you who are running from it. I know you, Keri Thomas; you're frightened to death of love!" he berated her. "You run from it!"

Keri pushed her hair from her face and looked directly at him. "You never said anything about love," she told him.

His dark brows contracted sharply. "How could I? You tend to bound off like a Texas jackrabbit if I get too close. For heaven's sake, couldn't you see how much I wanted you?"

Keri held out a hand to him, and he automatically helped her up. Her knees were a little weak, but she stood her ground. "Yes, I could see you wanted me—but love?" She shook her head.

His face softened. "Yes, *love*," he affirmed. "I tried to take it easy. Oh, I know I forced you to stay after your accident and then I had to come to Houston to get you, but that was because I didn't know how to conduct a long-distance affair. Like you said, that would be an unbearable strain. The only hold I had over you was passion."

Keri looked away from the smoldering fires in his eyes. His gentle finger under her chin brought her face back.

"Why the disappearing act tonight?" he asked.

GYPSY ENCHANTMENT

"I saw some girl hanging on your arm and . . ."—she closed her eyes—"I thought someday you would marry someone like her. I knew you would never love me. . . ."

"Oh, Keri," he ground out as his arms closed around her. "Little fool," he whispered into her hair. "Wait!" He put her from him and went to the desk.

He unlocked a drawer and removed a small package. Coming to her, he said very solemnly, "Will you marry me, Keri Thomas?"

Abruptly, her legs gave out on her, and Keri sat down heavily on the sofa, which luckily was behind her.

Reid opened the box and removed a ring. In its center was mounted a magnificent ruby, its glowing color accented by a circle of diamonds.

She gasped as he held it out to her, hers for the taking. "You can't want to marry me, Reid,"—she was begging him to be sensible—"I have no background. I come from very plain people."

"You are everything I want." He sat beside her, his thigh hard and warm beside her own. "Don't make me wait any longer. I've tried to give you little hints for weeks. Remember I told you we had unfinished business? I apologized for wanting to make you my mistress before and said that marriage didn't occur to me. Didn't you understand I was hinting at it then? Didn't you suspect when I followed you to Houston? I've been patient, Keri, trying not to scare you into running away again. Don't I deserve a reward?" he cajoled her with his winning ways.

He lifted her hand and slipped the ring on her finger while she sat there in a daze, not quite daring to believe.

"Are you sure this is what you want, really sure?" she asked in wobbly tones.

GYPSY ENCHANTMENT

He smiled seductively. "You are one difficult female to convince. Since the holidays are coming up, I thought we could combine our wedding and honeymoon with Christmas. Maybe you'll believe me when you see the wedding ring on your hand." He dropped his lashes in a dangerous leer. "Remember I said I was going to find a way to tie you to me? A gold band will do the trick. If it doesn't, well, I can get you pregnant and hide your shoes," he threatened with diabolical glee.

"Well, I . . . well, really, Reid," she spluttered.

His head bent to hers. "Say yes, darling," he encouraged.

"Yes, darling," she mimicked. Then she smiled, tears filled her eyes and she hid her face on his jacket.

"Salty rain?" he asked gently, teasing her a little. His voice had deepened. Now the leashed fire in his eyes was unbound. He stood, taking her with him. Holding her close, he walked out of the room and up the steps, neither of them seeing Milton's silent form as he locked up the house.

In the bedroom, t hey faced each other with new knowledge stretching like a young, tender vine between them, a realization of total commitment and love at long last come to fruition.

There was no hesitancy in Reid, no doubts, and only a lingering bit in Keri. She trusted this man as she had trusted no other person in her life.

This was life as it was meant to be, she thought as her lover pulled the tab of the zipper and the silk dress fell like a shower of flame at their feet. He picked it up, placing it almost with reverence on a chair, laying his coat and tie beside it.

He held out his cuffs for her to remove the links, which she did, and then she unfastened his buttons, too.

GYPSY ENCHANTMENT

"You're so lovely," he said as he removed one item after another from her until he had reached the desired goal. She resisted climbing into the bed until he was ready. She pushed him into a chair and knelt to untie his shoes.

Her eyes flashed darkly at him as she glanced up to find him studying her with an ardent hunger in his sea-colored eyes. "I've missed you," he said, and there was the loneliness of ten years in his voice.

After pulling off his shoes and socks, Keri put them aside and reached for his belt. Swiftly, she tugged him out of the pants, impatient to be with him.

"We wouldn't have made it before. We were too young," she told him. "I was scared. People have a way of disappearing or disappointing a person. Like Granny. Or Mack."

She stepped back, looking like a small goddess with her fiery dark eyes and curling riot of hair. A gasp was torn from his throat; he stooped, then lifted her proudly into his arms.

She swung her legs around his lean waist, locking her ankles behind him, and wrapped her arms around his strong shoulders as he carried her triumphantly across the room, setting her down carefully on the mattress.

He lost no time in establishing his claim as his hands moved in a long caress over her curving back and along her buttocks as she lay beside him. His body was rigid with masculine passion that he couldn't and had no intention of hiding from her.

Keri swept her hands over the furry mat of his chest; her foot rubbed up and down his hard leg, loving the feel of him, the absolute strength that was so gentle with her.

"Sweet gypsy," he murmured. "Come to me."

GYPSY ENCHANTMENT

Raising himself on his arms, he pressed for the ultimate contact and she willingly gave herself to his loving touch.

"I love you," she whispered.

He buried his face in the cloud of dark hair on the pillow. "That's the first time you've said it," he said.

"I've wanted to, often." She pressed her cheek to his, then, in wonder, searched along his face with her fingers. "Salty rain?" she asked, awed by her discovery.

"Tears, beloved," he admitted.

"For . . . for me?" She couldn't remember anyone ever crying for her.

His arms tightened around her, and his body covered hers protectively as if he would shut out the evil of the world from her. "For a young girl I never knew but that I love." He lifted his head to gaze with adoring eyes on his beloved. "She had such simple wishes—a red bicycle, piano lessons, someone to belong to. And when she didn't get them, it didn't turn her bitter or cold toward others. She grew up into a loyal, sweet woman. And I love that woman, too. More than I thought possible to love anyone, I love you."

His lips covered hers in a seal of promise. Her mouth opened under his, accepting all that he wanted to give her and giving all that she had in her of love in return.

He released her mouth and kissed along her cheeks where tiny dimples hid like bashful sunbeams.

"Your roaming days are over, gypsy," he told her in confident, happy tones like the sea murmuring in starlight.

"We can drop the 'i' from my name. I'm no longer

homeward bound. I'm home." She laid her hands on the strong arms that surrounded her. "In your arms, I'm home."

"So you are," he whispered, beginning the joyous task of re-creating the universe from the starburst of their passion. "And so am I."

Silhouette Desire

Six new titles are published on the first Friday every month. All are available at your local bookshop or newsagent, so make sure of obtaining your copies by taking note of the following dates:

OCTOBER 5th

NOVEMBER 2nd

NOVEMBER 30th

JANUARY 4th

FEBRUARY 1st

MARCH 1st

Silhouette Desire

Now Available

Late Rising Moon by Dixie Browning

Larain expected to get control of her life again as manager of Silas Flynt's art gallery. Instead the icy facade she cultivated melted completely as she abandoned herself in Silas' arms.

Without Regrets by Brenda Trent

Despite their vow never to part, Halette and Kale's blissful marriage had shattered. Now, amidst the splendours of the Orient, the old passions flared again, strong and steady, and challenged all their hesitations.

Gypsy Enchantment by Laurie Paige

Keri Thomas had left Louisiana and Reid Beausan to begin her life again in Houston. But on her return, the man who had stolen her innocence seduced her again, rekindling passions she had been desperate to forget.

Silhouette Desire

Now Available

Colour My Dreams by Edith St. George

When cool Robyn Stuart travelled to Fiji to lure artist Philip Holt back to civilization, she didn't expect to be seduced by the primitive pulse of the island—and discover her own primitive passions in the arms of its devastating inhabitant.

Passionate Awakening by Gina Caimi

Arden knew it was a chance in a lifetime when she was commissioned to write the biography of reclusive tycoon Flint Masters. But her objectivity gave way once Flint revealed his most private self to her—and his sudden interest in her as a woman.

Leave Me Never by Suzanne Carey

It was an honour to be accepted as a student under the great Dr. Benjamin Reno. But Terry had to fight her feelings for the man who had claimed her body and soul six years before—and whose eyes now burned with anger as well as passion.

Silhouette Desire

Coming Next Month

Fabulous Beast by Stephanie James

Before, Tabitha had only studied the elusive beasts of legend. Then she rescued Dev Colter from danger on a remote island and found that she had awakened a slumbering dragon

Political Passions by Suzanne Michelle

Newly-elected mayor Wallis Carmichael was furious to discover that sensual Sam Davenport was really a Pulitzer Prize-winning journalist. Politics and journalism don't mix—and now she had to find out if he was just another reporter out for a story.

Madison Avenue Marriage by Cassandra Bishop

Famous mystery writer Lily Lansden needed a "husband" for her winery commercial and Trent Daily fitted the bill. But when the game of pretend turned into real love could Lily give up her Madison Avenue marriage?

Silhouette Desire

Coming Next Month

Between the Covers by Laurien Blair

Everything changed between co-authors Adam and Haley when they began writing their ninth book together—a romance. Were they only playing out a story or were they friends now unleashing desires restrained for too long?

To Touch the Fire by Shirley Larson

Raine had loved Jade since she was sixteen— but he was her sister's husband. Now her sister had left him—would his bitterness and her guilt over the past threaten their awakening passions?

On Love's Own Terms by Cathlyn McCoy

Luke Ford had been out of Bonnie's life for seven years. But now her devastating husband wanted a second chance, and Bonnie's common sense was betrayed by a passion that still burned.

Silhouette Desire

THE MORE SENSUAL PROVOCATIVE ROMANCE

95p each

- 109 ☐ ONLY THIS NIGHT
  Suzanne Simms
- 110 ☐ DIAMOND GIRL
  Diana Palmer
- 111 ☐ THE HAWK AND THE HONEY
  Dixie Browning
- 112 ☐ TRIED AND TRUE
  Marie Nicole
- 113 ☐ MIXED DOUBLES
  Jasmine Cresswell
- 114 ☐ FRAGRANT HARBOUR
  Erin Ross
- 115 ☐ GAMBLER'S WOMAN
  Stephanie James
- 116 ☐ CONTROLLING INTEREST
  Janet Joyce
- 117 ☐ THIS BRIEF INTERLUDE
  Nora Powers
- 118 ☐ OUT OF BOUNDS
  Angel Milan
- 119 ☐ NIGHT WITH A STRANGER
  Nancy John
- 120 ☐ RECAPTURE THE LOVE
  Rita Clay
- 121 ☐ LATE RISING MOON
  Dixie Browning
- 122 ☐ WITHOUT REGRETS
  Brenda Trent
- 123 ☐ GYPSY ENCHANTMENT
  Laurie Paige
- 124 ☐ COLOUR MY DREAMS
  Edith St. George
- 125 ☐ PASSIONATE AWAKENING
  Gina Caimi
- 126 ☐ LEAVE ME NEVER
  Suzanne Carey

All these books are available at your local bookshop or newsagent, or can be ordered direct from the publisher. Just tick the titles you want and fill in the form below.

Prices and availability subject to change without notice.

SILHOUETTE BOOKS, P.O. Box 11, Falmouth, Cornwall.

Please send cheque or postal order, and allow the following for postage and packing:

U.K. – 50p for one book, plus 20p for the second book, and 14p for each additional book ordered up to a £1.63 maximum.

B.F.P.O. and EIRE – 50p for the first book, plus 20p for the second book, and 14p per copy for the next 7 books, 8p per book thereafter.

OTHER OVERSEAS CUSTOMERS – 75p for the first book, plus 21p per copy for each additional book.

Name ....

Address ....

....